PENGUIN BOOKS
SEVEN BOOKS FOR GROSSMAN

Morris Lurie lives in Melbourne, Australia.
Seven Books for Grossman is his sixteenth book.

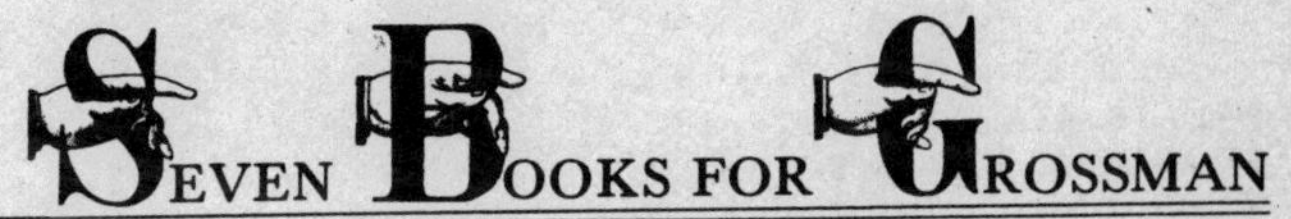

Seven Books for Grossman

Fiction by Morris Lurie

Penguin Books

Published with the assistance of the Literature Board
of the Australia Council

Penguin Books Australia Ltd,
487 Maroondah Highway, P.O. Box 257
Ringwood, Victoria, 3134, Australia
Penguin Books Ltd,
Harmondsworth, Middlesex, England
Penguin Books,
40 West 23rd Street, New York, N.Y. 10010, U.S.A.
Penguin Books Canada Ltd,
2801 John Street, Markham, Ontario, Canada
Penguin Books (N.Z.) Ltd,
182-190 Wairau Road, Auckland 10, New Zealand

First published by Penguin Books Australia, 1983

Copyright © Morris Lurie, 1983

Typeset in Baskerville by Dovatype, Melbourne

Made and printed in Australia
by Dominion Press Hedges & Bell

CIP

Lurie, Morris, 1938-   .
Seven Books for Grossman.
ISBN 0 14 006837 6.
I. Title.
A823'.3

Two parts of this book first appeared in
Australian *Penthouse* and one part in *Overland*
in somewhat different form.

Not for Anna C.,
but thanks all the same

The characters in this book are
entirely imaginary and bear no
relation to any living person,
though I should in all fairness say
that the character of Grossman
may owe more than a little
something to Zero Mostel's
performance in *The Producers*,
Robert Crumb's comic strip hero
Mr Natural, and – by far and away
my largest debt – the gorgeously
unruly behaviour of my own
many-years-departed dear old dad.

Ⓗouse abandoned, goods in secret storage, his two cars sold for a rapid song, Fielding, forty-two, a Professor of Literature, checked into a large hotel. His wife, under another name, was fled to another country, his children similarly disguised and dispersed. Fielding checked in wearing the clothes of a woman.

His skirt and jacket were classic Chanel, his silk blouse from Jaegar, his handbag and gloves and high-heeled pumps matching and authentic Gucci. He wore a Number 7 eyeliner by Elizabeth Arden with lashes colour-cued, his cheeks and lips were Helena Rubinstein, his scent Paco Rabanne.

A small amethyst set in platinum rode on the froth of silk over his Warners Formfit bra.

Fielding at the desk proffered the credit card of a compliant friend, his handbag flashing for calculating seconds the Super Tampax within – oh cunning Fielding! His Gucci glove enshrouded the tremble as he registered the borrowed name. That done, he followed the bellhop and his luggage (shark-grey Vuitton) to the elevator, stockings whispering, Fielding teetering gaily on his giddy heels.

His room was on the nineteenth floor. The bellhop put down his luggage, opened drapes, indicated the bathroom, switched on lights.

Fielding slipped out from his handbag the exactly correct tip.

The bellhop nodded.

The door closed.

Fielding stood alone.

'Hee hee,' he giggled, a naughty boy in a big man's world, all alone in a grand hotel.

But this was no time for horseplay.

He began to unpack.

He attended to his clothes quickly – the skirts, the blouses, the slither of stockings, the delicious underwear – and then he turned to the other case.

A ream of quarto bond.

A ream of quarto bank.

Carbon paper.

Pencils.

He unzipped and set out on the desk opposite the bed his portable typewriter, the selfsame

Olivetti Lettera 22 upon which, so many years ago, he had written his Master's thesis – oh sentimental magic.

The Golden Bowel: Anal Retentive Symbolism in the Fiction of Henry James.

His hand rested on it for a tender moment.

Thin-boned Fielding, wispy blonde-haired, pale blue-eyed: the quintessential WASP.

'Christ, it's hot in here,' he suddenly said.

He took off the Chanel jacket, stepped out of the Chanel skirt. The silk Jaegar blouse flapped. He took that off too.

'Ah,' said Fielding. 'That's better.'

Now, on the desk opposite the bed, he set out a line of books.

First, seven works of fiction.

Slaughterhouse-Five.

The Spinoza of Market Street.

The Old Man and the Sea.

archie and mehitabel.

The Catcher in the Rye.

As I Lay Dying.

The Kandy-Kolored Tangerine-Flake Streamline Baby.

Then three of reference.

Roget's Thesaurus.

Fowler's Modern English Usage.

The Pocket Oxford Dictionary.

From the bottom of the case he took a bottle of Scotch.

Opened it.

A carton of unfiltered cigarettes.

Tore off the cellophane.

Ashtray.
Lighter.
A glass.
Everything?
He made rapid inventory.
Everything.
Fielding closed his eyes.
Inhaled and exhaled a long shaky breath.
Then crossed himself quickly.
Fell to his knees.
'O Ernest, Isaac and William, Nobel Laureates all,' he intoned, his eyes still closed. 'O Kurt and Tom and J.D. and Don, yes, even Don. O writers of literature, O toilers in the field of the written word. Forgive me for what I am about to do.'
His mouth a grim line.
'But I do it for the reason that you yourselves toiled.'
His mouth grimmer still.
'Money.'
Fielding stood up.
'All right,' he said, addressing the desk, the Olivetti, the waiting white pages. 'Here's the whole sad story. Suckered by gangsters. Rigged wheel, marked deck, mirrors, the whole bag of tricks. Now they want their money – which I don't have in a leap year of Sundays – or me and mine are deader than death.'
Fielding shuddered.
'And one of them was a politician!' he suddenly howled.
From his handbag Fielding took a card, grimy

and much thumbed, propped it against his books, stared at it, read it over and over, his inspiration, his target, his mantra.

Grossman Press
Erotica for the Connoisseur

Now he was quick, efficient.

He wound paper into the typewriter, bond and bank, carbon between.

He poured and drank a deep finger of undiluted Scotch.

He lit and sucked greedily upon an unfiltered cigarette.

His hands positioned themselves over the typewriter keys.

And then he froze.

'Oh Jesus,' he said. 'What?'

Nothing.

The ashtray on the desk filled with butts.

The level in the Scotch bottle sank.

An hour.

An hour and a half.

Nothing.

A howling blank.

Fielding saw suddenly his innocent children, saw in exact close-up their trusting open smiles. His eyes lensed with tears.

'Come on,' he pleaded. 'Come on.'

Oh where were they, those creamy limbed lovelies who ran in his head day and night, so easily summoned, thrashing and wanton, slick with heat, angled and open in every conceivable – and then some – way?

Departed.

Fled.

Fielding's brain blanker than blank.

Desperate, deep into the second hour now, his throat stiff with Scotch and smoke, Fielding began to rummage through his personal history, the details of his own sexual life.

'Valerie!' he remembered.

Yes, Valerie, Valerie, bang-happy Val, already massive at fourteen under her stretched sweater, a legend in the neighbourhood, there wasn't a boy who hadn't at least copped a feel, and here was Fielding, just turned thirteen, copping with the best, her things sprung up right into his face, those mad guzzly bags, to which he'd attached himself feverishly as though here was the source of all mortal courage, twin fountains of audacity, come get your fill, and yes, suddenly courageous outside his years, heroic beyond measure, he'd reached for her skirt, and up it flew, shameless Val shamelessly assisting, and down came –

Skid marks.

'Oh do me do me!' cried bang-happy Val, white thighs springing apart like a flung-open encyclopedia in the school library. 'Oh do me do me I have to I don't care if I die!'

Skid marks on her underpants.

Which Fielding must have glimpsed for less than a second, a second at most, but that was enough, that did it, good clean WASP Fielding fled in horror, limp for the next six months.

Fielding, at his desk, fled to Veronica. His first. Yes, his very first. Actual physical penetration. His very first time actually in.

But wait a minute, Fielding remembered, it was awful, it was like doing it to sand, it was the driest thing in the whole world, a desert, a drought, and right through the entire hammering and battering shameful experience Veronica just lying there chattering gaily about the most gorgeous ming blue cashmere sweater she'd ever seen, oh it was heavenly, except, well, there was that scrumptious blush pink one too, and oh yes the darling mauve one, oh but Mumsy had a sort of mauve one so maybe she couldn't do that, she – 'Oh, you're not even *listening*!' she had suddenly said to Fielding, who that very second had actually and finally triumphed over the drought and managed – a miracle – to get it in.

'Oh shit,' moaned Fielding, feeling it die.

Fielding fled on.

'Audrey?' he attempted.

And one by one he went through them all, every girl, every woman, every wink, every nudge, every slightest feel, a frantic novice clicking his beads, the nurse, the statistician, the shop assistant, the student, the stewardess, the sloe-eyed translator with the black mole, but where Fielding sought to recall passion, wetness, openness, throbbing heat, wild flicking tongues and tearing gripping fingers and outrageous mad pelvic thrusts, what he encountered was otherwise.

Bad breath.

Rashes.

Groper's wrist.

Lounge lizard back.

Endless WASP guilt.

Fielding looked down at himself, where he hung in silk.

Nothing.

Less than nothing.

And so, at last, he summoned up his wife.

Elspeth.

Sweet darling Elspeth.

No jugs to speak of, but courageous nipples. They jumped up from the plain of her chest like a pair of baby's thumbs, Fielding's delight to flick them up and down like the settings on his Japanese cassette-deck, endlessly adjusting her for Dolby noise reduction, bias and chrome.

'Aha!' crowed Fielding, coming alive at last.

Quickly he snapped wide his panties to check how he was.

'Aw shit.'

You would have needed a microscope.

'Well, it's her fault!' he cried. 'She's so uptight! Never with the light on! Always in the dark! Holy Jesus, married fourteen years and I've never even seen my own wife's *downstairs gizmo*!'

Fielding jumped up, seething.

'I bought her open-crotch panties for her birthday, a fantasy in filigree black lace, she sewed them back up!'

He paced, furious.

'She won't even do it doggie fashion!'

His voice swelled with outrage.

'Never mind letting me wear my Groucho mask!'

Fielding strode to the wardrobe, flung it open.

The mirror within shimmered with light.

'Hello, big spender,' said Fielding to Fielding.

Brazen in bra, suspender belt and hose, bikini panties and high-heeled pumps.

'Slut,' said Fielding with a wink.

'Bitch,' lolling his tongue.

'Let's go, hot stuff,' said Fielding to Fielding, hooking thumbs into his panties, turning, bending, the tongue, the red lips, the lashed mascara-rimmed winking eye.

'OK?'

'OK.'

And now quickly he strides to his desk, primed at last, rife with images, a catalogue of desire, but his face studiously deadpan.

A fresh cigarette lit.

A gulp of Scotch.

And now, his hands on the typewriter keys, venting the odd fart to signify business, the Professor of Literature begins.

Listen:

The uncomfortable wedding gown in which Armalee Snoot née Crotchfeel had just been married was an heirloom. Yes, and the heavy lace-embroidered wedding gown was fastened with one hundred and eight tiny buttons in a row down the front. Yes, and each tiny cloth-covered button nestled inside a stiff cotton loop. Yes, and Nathaniel Snoot started on the top button of his brand new bride's heirloom wedding gown. Yes, and he couldn't undo it. Yes, and he couldn't undo the second button either. Yes, or the third. Yes, and Armalee sat patiently on the side of the bed in the motel, her arms by her sides.

Yes, and now Nathaniel Snoot asked his bride to stand up. Yes, and she did. Yes, and he said he would have to do it this other way. Yes, and Armalee said please don't tear anything; it's my Quaker great-great-great-grandmother's heirloom.

Yes, and listen:

Nathaniel Snoot bent down and began to work the tight heirloom wedding gown up to uncover Armalee's long legs. Yes, and when he got it to her knees it became extremely difficult. Yes, and Armalee stood with her arms by her sides while her brand-new husband worked. Yes, and Nathaniel Snoot got it past her knees and half way up her thighs. Yes, and now it was very hard indeed. Yes, and he kept going. Yes, and then he saw the white flash of the crotch of Armalee's cotton pants. Yes, and then there was a kind of pop as the stiff heirloom wedding gown jumped over Armalee's hips.

A kind of pop.

Now Nathaniel Snoot told his brand-new bride Armalee to lie down. Yes, and she did. Yes, and Nathaniel Snoot hooked all of his fingers into the elasticized waistband of Armalee's white wholesome cotton pants and pulled them down. Yes, and he pulled them past her shoes and continued to pull past the need to pull. Yes, and the pants sailed clear across the room and came to rest on the Gideon Bible on the small table underneath the framed seascape on the opposite wall.

Hi ho.

Grossman, in the flesh, was exactly as Fielding had envisioned:

The fat.

The sweat.

The stains.

The leering gold tooth.

'Yass?' said Mr Grossman, rising asthmatically from behind his desk.

Fielding faltered, almost took a step back.

'*Dirty Jew!*' hissed Fielding's WASP brain.

But Grossman noticed no faltering. Or were such reactions his common lot?

'Ah! Professor!' he cried, thick liverish lips widening the show of gold. 'Come in, come in!'

Fielding, collecting himself quickly, entered, in tweed. Tweed jacket, tweed tailored skirt. Oh very Burberry British, just a hint of ravishing lace beneath. His blouse was bone, the trim petite collar held in place with a stylishly simple Georg Jensen silver pin. Gunmetal stockings, seamed, of course. His shoes a modified golfing style with sensible heel, tasselled tongue, a whisper of brogue about the toe. And about his shoulders, loosely knotted, artfully careless, femininity finally proclaimed by an Yves St Laurent silk square, a flash of midnight blue cut through with bands of red and electric green. His scent was Patou's Joy.

'Take a seat,' said Grossman. 'Professor. Pliss.'

'Oh,' said Fielding, unprepared for the courtesy. 'Thank you.'

Fielding perched on the edge of the indicated hard wooden chair, unsure for a moment what to do with his legs.

He attempted a small smile.

Grossman responded in spades.

Beside the gold tooth was one that was black.

Fielding fled his eyes quickly around the room.

Fire-sale steel cabinets.

A dangling naked bulb.

A scarred blackened desk heaped and overflowing with grimy pages, flung-open phone books, a grease-banded black hat.

And right in the middle of it all, a plate stained with egg, a half-eaten onion, a glass that had once held milk.

Fielding repressed a shudder, shifting on his chair to touch even less of it. Oh the germs! The filth! God only knows the diseases that lurked here!

Fielding looked quickly down at his gloved grip on the zippered suede envelope wherein his manuscript rode on his tweed lap.

'Oh,' said Fielding. 'Well.'

He was, after all, here on business.

And quickly he unzipped, businesslike, brisk.

'Ah!' said Grossman, leaning forward, spying pages.

Fielding handed them across.

The ninety crisp pages he had written in three feverish days and nights in his hotel room, exhausted, starving, but too frightened to call roomservice, subsisting on chocolate bars, whisky, cigarettes, and anyhow too bound up in the fortunes of Nathaniel Snoot and Armalee Crotchfeel and all the other characters his maddened brain has sprung to life, Humbert Digit and Phoebe Sludge at the local condom factory, Madame Vulv and her Coitus Circus, the lesbians in the Triflemore Motel – where Nathaniel Snoot had stepped into a time warp and disappeared for fifteen years – and the final scene with the department store Santa and the little girl, and all in the aw shucks, simple wisdom, so easy to read style of Kurt 'Slaughterhouse-Five' Vonnegut, in Professor of Literature Fielding's view – and he lectured on him – a profound phoney, and what a choice revenge.

'*Jailbait Fifteen*?' read Grossman. 'Hmmm.'

And began to read.

Now Fielding knew what would happen next, could see it as exactly as he had envisioned Grossman himself. And more than Grossman. The building, the lobby, the office, the scarred blackened desk.

All of which, in a sense, he had had from Reuben Rabinowitz, of course, though Rabinowitz had not actually described.

Well, not in so many words.

Professor Rabinowitz, university colleague, still unmarried at forty-four, and no plans in that direction either, a curly-haired seven-o'clock-shadowed perennial playboy, forever talking about poon. He had no other topic. Poon was his Major and all else besides. An enthusiast. An authority. A specialist in the field. 'Boy, did I have me some poon last night,' was how he began every day. 'Air hostess poon. And you can't fly any higher than that.' Around lunchtime he would become pensive, fretful, his eyes darkening with longing and lust. 'Boy, am I hungry for poon,' he would moan. 'Any size, any shape. Long as it's genuine poon.' But then, five o'clock, five-thirty, he would make some phonecalls, low whispered talk, and hang up bushy-tailed, eager, his movements quick as mercury. His eyes would flash, alive again. 'Got my poon waiting,' he would cry, rubbing his hands excitedly together. 'Hot from the oven. Wet and deep. Night, all!' And then suddenly discovered being outrageously personal with two boys at once in the back row of the local movie house. Good students, too, both of them. Fielding was shocked. Shocked and disgusted. A Jewish homosexual. He had never before heard of such a thing.

'*Dirty Jew!*' Fielding had thought.

But from Rabinowitz, before he was blown – yes, the boys had been active too – the name of Grossman. A grubby card handed across. Grossman Press. A phone number. The address.

'He's hard, but he's fair,' Rabinowitz had said. 'A flat fee, no royalties. In that business, that's standard. Leave the pseudonym to him. He knows the market. What do you want, fame? Go somewhere else. This is for money, pure and simple.'

And then, with a curly-haired blue-cheeked cherubic smile, 'I did mine for a lark.'

Of course.

So Fielding had phoned, made an appointment. Wondered should he explain the circumstances necessitating the clothes in which he would appear – the gangsters, the gambling debts, the fear for his life. Decided no. Rather, couldn't for some vague reason form the words. Speaking not to Grossman, but to a girl, a woman, a female voice. Grossman's secretary, Fielding surmised.

'Strumpet,' Fielding thought, hanging up.

He caught a cab. The address was on the other side of the city, a dubious locale, best avoided at night. Fielding extracted a Dunhill Superior Mild filtered cigarette from a tapestried cigarette case, fitted it to a long rhinestoned holder, smoked.

The cabdriver attempted conversation. Fielding cut him icily dead.

He would not be there for thirty minutes, thirty minutes at least, but already he could see the building exactly. It would by anywhere from sixty to ninety years old. Grimy. Grey. The names and businesses in the lobby directory vague and anonymous, the perspex letters falling out, like gaps in teeth. The lobby would have a black and white tiled floor, the tiles cracked and broken, gritty underfoot. A litter of cigarette ends. Newspapers. Worse.

Fielding was not disappointed.

Grossman Press was on the fourth floor. Handy

for quick stairway escapes. Fielding rode up in the elevator. A reeking mop stood in a metal bucket just inside the metal grille you pulled across to make the elevator move. Fielding smiled, delighted with the detail. The elevator groaned, moving slowly up.

Four.

The elevator stopped with a tooth-jarring clang. Fielding pulled open the grille.

But now there was a surprise, a detail Fielding had got completely wrong. For the voice he had spoken to over the phone, making his appointment, belonged not to some hardened strumpet, lacquered with paint, reeking of cheap scent, bosomy, sagging, as tough as a brick, but to a fresh-faced girl surely no more than eighteen. If anything younger. Her skin glowed, her lips soft and red, but unmarked by make-up, Lux-scrubbed, her shiny brown hair fell to her shoulders in a natural wave, the softest golden haze burnished her bare forearms, her nails were unpainted, and trimmed sensibly short.

She was Audrey Hepburn in *Roman Holiday*.

She was the young Mia Farrow.

She was the essence of innocence, virginity proclaimed.

Fielding, in his tweed, felt himself blush, a coarse harlot before such fresh youth.

The girl delicately dropped her eyes.

Oh silken lashes.

Then Fielding found voice, introduced himself.

'Oh yes,' said the girl, finding with a finger his

name in her appointments book. 'Professor Fielding.'

Her soft lips opened onto perfect white teeth.

'Just one moment, Professor Fielding,' she said, skipping up from her desk, dancing to a door, gently tapping.

Fielding noting her demure white blouse.

Her simple grey skirt.

Her black unfussy shoes with just a hint of a heel.

'Of course,' Fielding thought. 'He wouldn't have a brazen strumpet. Much too obvious. And somehow not quite perverted enough. But, even so, this girl . . .'

'You can go in now, Professor Fielding,' the girl said to him, with an encore of that wonderfully fresh innocent smile.

Fielding went in.

'*Dirty Jew*!' hissed his brain, Grossman first seen, in the flesh at last, Fielding faltering.

But also rejoicing.

Oh, how wonderful.

Grossman.

Wonderful down to the last dirty detail.

The face, the jowls, the lips, the tiny wet pink eyes – these behind steel-rimmed eyeglasses so thick his eyes loomed and diminished like fish in a bowl, until, with a movement of his head, Grossman pulled down the curtain, the lenses turned opaque.

Fielding swallowed with difficulty.

He was bald on top, bald and shiny, but there was black hair everywhere else, sprouting from his ears, from his nose, running like fire along the tops of his gross, heavy hands, right down the fingers too, rampant and unruly, the fingers marvels in themselves, sausages of fleshy stumpiness, and just how massively meaty you could gauge from the pinkie of the right, where a rounded gold ring bit in like a vice, the fat flesh jumping up tumultuously on either side.

Oh, he was perfect, perfect.

The very essence of dirty Jew.

The pornographer supreme.

And now Fielding moved to his clothes.

The inkgreen shirt, bad taste and scent of evil in ultimate combination, a gangster colour, Mafia, the peaks of the collar mangled and pointing like the horns of a bull, and under the arms the foul colour even darker, sour and unwashed.

The boots, just this side of orthopaedic, broken laces, leather lumps, blue-veined white flesh gaping horribly above.

And the trousers.

Oh the trousers.

They were beyond colour, a sea of flecks and spots and stains, voluminous in their pleating, of that age before zippers and yes, a button brazenly undone, a hernia-sized lump riding beneath. And to the side of it, in that sea of flecks and spots and stains, the largest stain of all, curiously the exact shape of South America, yes, the entire continent, from the Panama Canal to the tip of Tierra del Fuego, and topographically correct too, bulging up at the Andes, a wetness for the rain forests of Brazil, arid and flat along the Patagonian plain. And around it all, banding the detailed inlets and passages of egress of each river and stream, the encrusted reticulation of the flowing saltine tides.

Fielding gulped in spellbound horror.

'So,' said Grossman, smiling warmly.

Fielding hastily handed across his work.

Grossmen read.

And now Fielding knew exactly what would happen. A dozen times at least his mind had played out the horrible scene.

Fielding steeled himself.

For Grossman would read slowly, painfully, for each word moving those thick liverish lips. And he would wheeze. And he would burp. He would plunge a finger into his ear. He would fart.

'Oh, the dirty little Jew,' Fielding thought. 'And what a pervert. He hasn't even mentioned my clothes.'

Yes, Fielding could see it all. Grossman would read, fingering his ear, fingering his nose, those vast hair-filled nostrils, burping, farting, gas from both ends, moving those thick liverish asthmatic lips, but finally he would finish. A silence then. A wheeze. But at last he would look up at Fielding. He would give a small smile. And then, with a grunt, he would stand.

Fielding closed his eyes.

For Grossman now would slowly unbutton those hideous trousers, take out his member – 'His *shlong*,' Fielding thought, shuddering, referring back to conversations with colleague Rabinowitz

– lay it down, beside the egg-stained plate, beside the half-eaten onion, beside the milk-besmirched glass, on the desk. Oh, Fielding could see it, could see it exactly – veined with purple, lying there like a dead eel.

And again Grossman would smile.

'Professor,' he would say. 'Say hello to your reader. When he stands up, you've got a hit.'

Fielding and Grossman both would look down at the lifeless length.

'Oh dear Mother of God,' Fielding silently prayed, his hands trembling inside their gloves.

He wanted a cigarette, he needed a cigarette, he was desperate for a cigarette, but he knew he couldn't manage it.

He saw his wife, his fresh young children.

Fielding was on the brink of tears.

'Oh, charming, charming,' Grossman said.

Fielding looked quickly up.

'Wonderful,' said Grossman, turning a page. 'Very novel, very nice.'

Fielding blinked.

It was unbelievable.

He stared at Grossman's fingers, those fat hairy tubes, saw them moving with surprising daintiness, touching the pages so lightly, an awed collector holding a Gutenberg Bible, a priceless jewel.

'Ah,' said Grossman, reading. 'Very elegant, very cleverly turned.'

And the lip-smacking? The nose? The ear? The burp? The fart?

Grossman sat in his chair as graceful as Fred Astaire, as impeccable as an English king, reading Fielding's manuscript with joy and respect.

'Beautiful,' said Grossman. 'Truly beautiful.'

It was unbelievable.

And he was quick. In thirty minutes it was done.

'Ah,' he said, putting down the last page. 'What a pleasure that was. What a joy.'

He smiled up at Fielding, and then bashfully down, as though in awe of such talent.

'Very clever,' Fielding thought, rallying quickly. 'Very clever. What an act. Bloody Jews. You have to hand it to them. And now, having flattered me in his slimy way, he'll beat me down, make me haggle, force me to grovel in front of him before he peels off some greasy notes and flings them in my face. Dirty little Jew!'

Grossman stood up.

Fielding quickly the same.

Grossman opened a drawer.

'Thank you, Professor,' he said. 'A pleasure to deal with you.'

And handed Fielding a brick of fifties so new they were like glass in Fielding's hand.

And twice the amount, at least, that Fielding had imagined in his wildest dreams.

Fielding was speechless.

Grossman bowed.

And then bowed again, showing him to the door.

Fielding began to cross to the elevator.

The secretary at her desk glowing with freshness, smiling like a rose.

Fielding smiled in return, pressing the button to go down.

And then Grossman spoke again.

'Oh, Professor?' he called lightly.

Fielding turned.

'I wonder if next time,' said Grossman, his voice a poem, 'we could have just a little bit more . . . *twat*?'

Grossman's smile the epitome of politeness.

'If it's not too much trouble.'

But the eyes like death.

'Professor.'

An Homage to Stravinsky

The rabbi of Pizlykca, Reb Nahum Goldbricker, paced to and fro in his study, tugging his side locks and smiting his breast. In the next room lay his daughter, Liebe Raizeleh, known to her school friends as Samantha, heaving and moaning and uttering deep sighs. For four weeks now her ripe seventeen-year-old body had been giving house room to a dybbuk. The foul imp raged like a fire deep inside her, impossible to dislodge. 'Oh, you brute, you brute!' Reb Nahum heard his daughter cry through the thin wall. 'Faster! Faster!'

Reb Nahum paced and paced, between tugs and smites muttering feverish snatches of Torah, Gemara, Mishnah, Midrash, and other holy texts, including

Henry Miller and the Kamasutra. What is truth? he asked himself. From whence comes goodness? What proof is there of an after-life? How tall is the devil exactly? Is there a God and is He well hung? 'Oh! Oh!' moaned his daughter through the thin wall, setting up a commotion in the rabbi's breast almost impossible to contain. 'Don't stop!' he heard her cry. 'For God's sake don't stop!'

A cricket sang its song behind the oven. Beyond the window stuffed with rags a wagon creaked. Pigeons cooed. Crows cawed. Swallows returned from warm climes and began to nest under the eaves. In the marketplace peddlers peddled, beggars begged, gossips gossiped, and whatever else is necessary to fill up this paragraph.

'Enough!' cried Reb Nahum Goldbricker. 'Four weeks is enough! I'm going in!'

Liebe Raizeleh lay almost naked on the bed, her hair dishevelled, her milky brow strung with sweat like tiny glistening pearls. Her struggles with the dybbuk had caused her coverings to fall to the floor and her nightdress to ride up, revealing not only her long maidenly legs but also that very place, God forbid, where the dybbuk had jumped in and taken up residence.

Reb Nahum took one look and fell at once to his knees, tugging and smiting for all he was worth, his lips a blur of invocation and prayer and also of regret that he hadn't brought his Instamatic camera.

'Out, dybbuk, out!' he shouted.

'Oh, out, dybbuk, out,' sang back the dybbuk in camp falsetto.

'What?' said Reb Nahum, opening one eye.

'Oh, deeper, deeper, you mad thing!' cried Liebe Raizeleh, and Reb Nahum saw the distressed girl, her eyes blank and glazed, attempting to pluck out the slippery imp from where he was lodged with the first two fingers of her right hand, plunging and plunging, in feverish pursuit.

The commotion in Reb Nahum Goldbricker's breast grew even more tumultuous, and lower.

And then Reb Nahum remembered with joy in his heart that God, may the angels on high sing His praises for evermore, had granted him not a daughter but a stepdaughter, a blessing indeed.

'Very well, dybbuk,' he said, straightening up. 'It's time to play my secret card. Move that hand, Liebe Raizeleh,' he said, unbuttoning with speed. 'Make way for the Ram's Horn!'

But if Fielding desired grossness, true Grossness, dirty Jew behaviour unalloyed and unadorned, desired it, required it, needed that strictest conformity to type, on his second visit to the pornographer he was not disappointed. He got it. Oh did he get it. Got it in spades, his cup filled thrice and grandly overflowing, grossness and coarseness and vile semitic uncouthness beyond the wildest measure of his milky WASP dreams.

Grossman greeted him at the door with a trench warfare fart.

A pickle factory burp.

Oh, he was filled with them, was Grossman, both noisome and noxious, from this end, from that, a blatant defiance of the Geneva Convention ruling on poison gas.

All that for starters.

Now came a catarrhal rearrangement of nasal phlegm, a sound of sludgy sluicegates, a drowning in the throat.

And then a grander performance, a proper nose blow, but skip the handkerchief, this done with the fingers, a pressure to the left nostril, to the right, a shake, a further squeeze, red-faced Grossman leaning right forward to avoid the splash.

'Oy!' cried Grossman, giving to the fingers a shake in the air, a wipe on his leg. 'Dat's better!'

And then, without further preamble, snatching from Fielding – yes, with that same hand, that hand just used – his manuscript, Fielding's offering today a savage mockery of Jewish Nobel Laureate Isaac Bashevis Singer, that chronicler of small town Jewish life in the Poland of long ago, Fielding bearding the lion in its own den, as it were, showing who's boss, calling the shots.

'How do you like that, Jewboy?' Fielding silently exulted. 'I've lampooned one of your own!'

Grossman, grabbing, emitted a tumult of gases.

Fielding, gagging, retreated to a chair.

But Grossman, reading, was just as vile.

For now a finger dived into an ear.

Twisted, inspected, its load of gold wiped on the knee.

Then instantly into the nose.

Fielding shuddered as Grossman clumsily licked this ear and nose finger to facilitate the turning of a manuscript page.

Grossman's thick lips making the while a clammy sound of chewing, a semi-dry smacking as he strenuously read.

Then Grossman suddenly diving a hand round the back, and digging deep, his face instantly mirroring the fiery red of an inflamed haemorrhoidal condition.

'When I'm finished here,' grunted Grossman, working like a maniac, 'these underpants you can take out and shoot!'

Applauding his own wit with a gas-bubble laugh.

Fielding sat frozen, a gaping fish.

But impossible to look away.

For if Grossman's grossness was as Fielding had desired, albeit of larger measure, his clothes today were otherwise.

Forget the sweaty shirt, the stained trousers, the cracked thick-leathered boots.

Grossman today was in pink.

Completely in pink.

A pink leotard.

Pink tights.

A pink tu-tu, the concertinaed folds of stiff tulle

standing horizontal from Grossman's ungainly girth.

Pink slippers, ballerina blocked, laced with pink ribbons, crisscrossed Grecian style over Grossman's lugubrious calves.

And on his head a silver tiara, this made from a cut-out silver star stapled to a silver band circling Grossman's huge bald dome.

On a corner of Grossman's strewn desk rested a silver-painted stick, to which was affixed, at one end, echoing the tiara, a tinsel-shiny, six-pointed, cut-out cardboard silver star.

Grossman's fairy wand.

'Well, I'm not saying a word about any of it,' Fielding silently vowed, 'unless he mentions mine first.'

And Fielding today was worth a mention. He was in a Laura Ashley, accommodating himself to an afternoon of unseasonal warmth: a billowing cotton of harvest blooms printed on a bed of fresh green. His shoes and handbag were basketweave white, his hat a sloppy wagonwheel of like texture and hue. Nude seamless stockings. Crisp elbow-length cotton white gloves. A splash of Revlon's Charlie, a youngish scent.

Grossman finished, farted, and arose.

He put the manuscript down.

He lifted up his arms.

He raised himself on his slippered points.

Then, wrists curved inwards over his head, fingers splayed and falling in artistic droop, his wood-blocked toes clattering out no known metronomic time on the carpetless office floor, he executed a tight, clumsy circle, a wobbly pirouette.

Fielding blinked, open-mouthed.

Grossman curtsied, the tu-tu rising like an aureole behind.

Then Grossman smiled bashfully, his cheeks pink, it was almost a blush, and then suddenly he began to tap and slap his body, the hips, behind, his breast, left and right. Then stopped, froze. Frowned, looked lost, confused. Ah! Of course! His smile to Fielding this time apologetic, meek. He held up an index finger. One minute. Wait. Now off he danced again, the tu-tu fluttering, the points clattering, tiny little steps, to a tall steel locker standing against a wall, which, opened, revealed a long black overcoat, shiny gaberdine.

Fielding blinked as Grossman fossicked in the pockets, here, there, inside, before at last turning, sounding a cry of 'Ah!'

Fielding saw money, a fat rubber-banded greasy roll.

Still on his points, Grossman danced back to Fielding, stood above him, wheezing slightly, his heart plainly sounding pit-a-pat.

Fielding mesmerized by the fingers peeling and flicking.

Grossman offered.

Fielding accepted.

Tucking it away quickly into his handbag, uncounted.

For some reason embarrassed.

Grossman curtsied low.

Fielding made to rise from his chair.

'Ah, Professor?' Grossman said.

Fielding froze.

'You have a minute?'

'Well, sure . . .' Fielding said. 'That is . . .'

Grossman beamed.

'Ah, you Professors,' he said. 'I know you Professors. Night writers, each and every one.'

And, still beaming, he bent down and gave to Fielding's right cheek a sudden playful pinch.

'Ha, boychick?' Grossman said, adding to the pinch a little twist. 'Burning the midnight oil, ha? Not so?'

And before Fielding could reply, could react in any way, flew away, quickly, dancing on his points, to the door.

'Oh, Miss Barthelmess?' he whispered out, the door opened no more than a crack, ballerinaed pink Grossman hidden behind. 'Could we have please two coffees? Oh, and listen, maybe a couple Danish also, I think the cheese.'

Now Grossman sat down, opposite Fielding, Grossman still beaming, Fielding trying for a polite smile.

Both sitting thus in silence.

Until the door tapped, Grossman quickly arose, and was back in a moment with the coffee and the pastries, all neat in paper cups and plates on a small pink plastic tray.

'A darling gel, that Miss Barthelmess,' Grossman remarked, slurping and munching. 'One in a million.'

Fielding, sipping delicately, with his eyes agreed.

'Vell, I don't know,' Grossman said, his coffee and Danish despatched, wiping his thick lips with the back of a hairy hand. 'Some days, some days. Phew. First, the printer. Then, the binder. Then, the distributor. And each one with his troubles and woes. I tell you, I haven't had a minute to myself all day. This is the first time I have had a chance to properly sit down.'

Fielding nodded with what he hoped was commiseration.

'Whoosh,' said Grossman. 'The price of paper.'

'Is that so?' Fielding ventured.

'The unions.' Grossman shook his head. 'The Arabs.'

'Indeed,' Fielding allowed.

'Sometimes I wonder,' Grossman said. 'I really do.'

Grossman, head nodding, lips pursed, his brows drawn down in a serious frown, lost himself for a long moment in private rumination, Fielding frowning too, unsure of his role in all this.

'Oy yoy yoy,' moaned Grossman softly, rocking on his seat.

'Why, I do believe he's lonely,' Fielding declared to himself.

The moaning dropped away.

Silence stretched.

Until Fielding felt it his obligation to speak.

'Well!' he began, chipper and cheery, surprising himself with his tone. 'You've certainly chosen a curious, um, *profession*, Mr Grossman.'

'Absolutely,' said Grossman, nodding his head. 'Absolutely. Never was said a truer word.'

Fielding leaned forward, smiling encouragement.

'But tell me, Mr Grossman,' he said. 'How did you, I mean, what made you . . .?'

Grossman shrugged.

'This business?' he said. 'Don't ask me. Listen. One brother I've got a brain surgeon, another one on the stock exchange, a mint of money, two sisters a judge.' Grossman tapped his chest with a suddenly strident finger. 'And I was always the clever one!'

Now Grossman leaned forward too.

'Look,' he said. 'Listen. One thing I've learnt. It doesn't matter in this life what you do. This, that, what's the difference? The important thing is –' Grossman looked hard at Fielding, imparting this knowledge – 'Get out of the house!'

Fielding bowed to the wisdom.

'Look,' said Grossman. 'This publishing the pornography, it's not so bad. I meet a lot of people, different types, all sorts. It's refreshing. You've got no idea. Well, maybe not all of them quite so nice . . .'

Grossman stood up, clasped his hands behind his back, paced a few paces.

'Oh, I get some cookies,' Grossman said. 'Some real cookies. For instance, last week. Someone had with me an appointment, a new chap. Hokay. Now it just so happened I was standing like this, the hands clasped behind, a few minutes peace, gazing from the window, looking out, looking down, fellow humanity passing in the street, thinking my private thoughts. I saw him pull up. A Rolls Royce. And not just a Rolls Royce, but with his initials in gold on the side. And not just the initials, but with a chauffeur too, with a cap, with the white gloves. The whole thing. Well, in he comes. The two of them. He's brought the wife.'

Grossman rolled his eyes.

'Thin!' he cried. 'You've never seen such thin! If she had a tittie, anywhere on her body, I didn't notice. And a tushie! Listen! You could have put it in an eggcup, and still have place for the egg!'

Grossman held up a finger.

'Wait,' he said. 'That was nothing. Him too. The thinness! The elegance! A positive prince! I tell you, next to him, even Cary Grant would look like a bum!'

Up went the finger again. There was more.

'All right,' said Grossman. 'I sat down. They sat down. I read what he's brought me. This gentleman. This prince. With the Rolls Royce, with the chauffeur, with the thin wife. Phew!' Grossman shook his head in remembered disbelief. 'On page one, he's bopping a post box, right in the mail slot. On page two, it's the exhaust pipe on a heavy diesel truck. On page three, he's stealing into the Louvre, he's taking a razor blade, he's making a slit in a major work of art – *a blowjob with the Mona Lisa*!'

Grossman flung out exasperated arms.

'I farmed it out to a competitor,' he said. 'What else could I do?'

Fielding had no reply.

'Ah, Professor!' Grossman cried, dancing in again, poised to give a second cheek pinch, but changing it at the last moment to a light tapping pat. 'What a pleasure you are! What a nice boychick! Even the typing is like a poem! Oh, if only they were all like you.'

Fielding lowered his eyes.

A silence again stretched.

Then Grossman suddenly held up a finger.

'An Homage to Stravinsky,' he solemnly announced.

Grossman took up the silver-starred wand. Raised himself on his ballerina points. The chin lifted. A flutter of fingers, establishing the mood. And gravely, at first slowly, but with a mounting momentum, his thick body moving with a lumpy grace, Grossman began to dance.

Glissades.

Pliés.

Echappés and *arabesques.*

All the classical movements, Grossman in flow from one to the next.

And then faster, *jetés*, Grossman's tiara-topped face crimson with effort and shiny with sweat, a glistening, fiery cannonball, his breath stentorian, his knee joints cracking around the room like artillery fire, around and around the room he went, anointing each corner with his silver-starred wand, Fielding sitting in dazed awe.

The dance completed, Grossman curtsied, a dying swan.

Fielding found his hands together in applause.

Both smiling bashfully.

'Here,' said Grossman, pushing out more notes. 'Take, take! To tell you the truth, Professor, I was a naughtie boy before.' He looked down at his blocked slippers, shuffling them awkwardly. 'I shortchanged you a bit.'

Grossman's face was a chastened cherub.

'Hey, he's not such a bad chap,' Fielding thought. 'I mean, for a Jew.'

'So . . .' said Grossman, sitting heavily down.

'Well . . .' said Fielding.

They smiled in silence.

'But Professor!' cried Grossman suddenly. 'You haven't even *touched* your Danish!'

'No . . . I . . .' Fielding began.

'May I?' said Grossman, hand hovering.

'Certainly!' cried Fielding. 'Help yourself! Please!'

'Ah, thank you, thank you!' cried Grossman, swooping it up. 'Very kind of you.'

Fielding smiled.

Grossman gobbled.

'Well . . .' said Fielding, arranging his handbag, straightening a glove.

'Of course, of course!' said Grossman, rising at once. 'You're a busy man! I've taken so much time! I'm sorry!'

'No, no,' said Fielding quickly. 'It's quite all right. I've enjoyed talking to you.'

'One minute!' cried Grossman. 'I'll show you to the door.'

Grossman dancing off quickly and taking from a peg an ancient dressing gown, a faded plaid based on burgundy.

Fielding looked discreetly elsewhere as Grossman hid away the pink.

Now Grossman opened wide the door.

'Until next time, Professor,' he said, offering a hand.

Fielding took it firmly.

Miss Barthelmess, at her desk, smiled at such cameraderie and cheer.

'Oh, and don't worry, Mr Grossman,' said Fielding, his voice stage whispering in filthy leer. 'My next manuscript will have *a terrific amount of twat*!'

Grossman looked aghast.

Miss Barthelmess blushed crimson.

Fielding, ashen, fled.

French Mustard

He was an old man who fished alone in a skiff in the Gulf Stream and he had gone eighty-four days now without the benefaction of a puta. *In the first forty days a boy had been with him. But after forty days without a* puta *the boy's parents had told him that the old man was now definitely and finally* loco cojones, *which is more distressing than wearing tin underpants. 'Did he obscenity in the milk of any untoward personal passage?' the father of the boy asked him again and again. The boy began to cry. It made the boy sad to see the old man come in each day with the mast of his manhood still unused. Furled, it looked like the flag of permanent defeat.*

The old man was thin and gaunt with deep wrinkles in the back of his neck and bore no resemblance to the actor Spencer Tracy. His hands had the deep-creased scars from handling heavy women in restrictive spaces with the meter ticking. But none of these scars was fresh. They were as old as the pudenda of the ancient whores behind the shark factory which even these the old man could no longer afford.

Everything about him was old save for the mast of his manhood which was a proud purple at the tip and then along its fine length strong and brown and decently blotched and knowing. The cojones *of the old man were like hills like white elephants except they were not that colour.*

'Pilo,' the boy said to him as they climbed the bank from where the skiff was hauled up. 'I could go with you again.'

The old man had taught the boy much fishy business and the boy loved him.

'No,' the old man said. 'You're with a lucky boat which catches much puta. *Stay with them.'*

'But remember how you went eighty-seven days without a puta *and then you had big ones every day for three weeks.'*

'I remember,' the old man said, remembering the last one, the Americano touristica, *the smell of alimony rich about her skin and still with the tricks and skill and high cunning in her hooker's box despite her advancing years, and screaming in his good ear all those fine places where she craved to be touched, Tiffany's, Saks Fifth Avenue, The Four Seasons, Bergdorf Goodman, until with a cry of Gucci she was finally landed, long and*

white and beautiful and noble, and then she awoke to take snap camera Polaroid pictures of his mast in the manner of all Americano touristicas, and then she took out her Japanese silicon-chip calculator and beat him down on the price of his fish, and the memory of all this stirred the old man inside his trousers patched with flour sacks until walking became difficult and the boy had to wait.

'Pilo,' said the boy. 'Is it the thing again of the arthritis?'

'Bugger the arthritis,' said the old man, throwing the prose style right out the window. 'Drop those shorts.'

Fielding today brash and glossy, brooking no crap. Hands plunged into the side pockets of electric purple velvet baggies, strutting impatiently on high silvery vinyl heels, a swinging shoulderbag to match. Oh colourful Fielding. The Fiorucci blouse, a pattern of Uncle Tom grinning golliwogs on a blaze of bright yellow. The short jacket Fiorucci too, mad with every colour under the sun, the flaring lapels crammed and crowded with badges, brooches, all manner of cheap disco tat: a palm tree, a pussy cat, a Save the Whale, a Vote for Nixon, and, best of all, a tiny pair of shiny pink plastic legs, salaciously gaping, the supremely realistic gizmo within on complete open show, and when you bent to look, a squeeze of the hidden water-filled rubber bulb and you got it smack in the eye.

'Come on there, gramps,' snapped Fielding, tossing his mod Afro high hennaed frizz. 'Time's movin', time's flyin' on!'

Fielding's jaws slapping around gum, framing a bubble with whore-red lips, choo-chooing to raucous music coming from somewhere close, filling Grossman's room, hard bop, driving, drumming jazz.

'Oh, git 'long there, gramps,' crooned Fielding, popping hot fingers in time to the jazzy beat. 'Rassle that ass.'

And Grossman?

Strangely subdued today, strangely subdued.

Sitting hunched and small, in an ancient Norfolk jacket elbowed with worn leather, his trousers the widest wale corduroy bags. Bunion-bunching sandals. Around his throat a lumpy woollen scarf. And on his head a dusty black Basque beret, tugged down all around, unjauntily straight.

'You awake there, gramps?' Fielding sang, sashaying in.

Grossman looked meekly up from the manuscript in his hand, Fielding's malicious slaughter of the once-great Hemingway, that great braggart, literature's bag of wind, also hunter, fisherman, relentless killer of wildlife supreme, duck, marlin, elephant, antelope, if it moved he bagged it, and look at him now, the tables turned, what an easy target.

Slowly he raised his eyeglasses to his brow.

Grossman's eyes revealed pink and moist.

'What is it, gramps?' Fielding lunged forth. 'Piles playin' up again? Haw haw!'

Grossman smiled weakly.

Dabbed with a ball of handkerchief his liquid eyes.

Slowly shook his head.

'Oh, those days,' whispered Grossman.

'What days?' spat out Fielding, impatiently boogying to and fro, back and forth. 'Come on there, man, speak up. Blow it out yore ass!'

'The twenties,' mumbled Grossman. 'The twenties in Paris.'

'What?' howled Fielding. 'Paris? Paris *what*?'

'Paris, France,' Grossman breathed.

'Aw, come on!' Fielding scoffed. 'Paris friggin' France! Big deal!'

Fielding, suddenly tiring of his gum, shot it expertly over his right shoulder, leering with satisfaction when he heard it strike metal somewhere with a bullseye *ping*!

Grossman continued to sit and nod and dab.

'Now listen,' Fielding said, legs spread and braced, hands arrogantly on hips, face thrust down to outstare any opposition. 'Ya've read my story, so give me the money, man, then, like – *Split-City*! Come on, I've got things to do.'

From Grossman, a sigh.

'Now, come on,' Fielding threatened. 'The

twenties! Paris friggin' France! I don't know. Modern times, man, modern times!' he suddenly shouted. 'Get with it!'

'I was there,' Grossman said quietly.

'Aw, shit,' Fielding sneered, spinning away, lighting a cigarette.

'Fitzgerald, Hemingway, Picasso, Gertrude Stein,' Grossman murmured. 'Miller, Nin, Joyce also. I knew them all.'

'Sure ya did, old man,' Fielding said. 'Sure ya did.' And then, his face instantly altering, all friendliness gone, pushing out a hand, palm uppermost, fingers grasping, 'Listen, the money, the loot, the bread!'

But the gesture wasted on Grossman, lost in a private litany. 'The Dome. The Select. The Deux Magots,' he continued, his voice easing out in a whisper, almost inaudible in the still-booming raucous jazz.

Fielding had to bend an ear.

'Oh, that café life,' intoned Grossman. 'That Left Bank.'

'Yeah, yeah,' Fielding mocked. Adding, in a meant-to-be-heard aside, 'Gold-plated phoney!'

Grossman suddenly chuckled.

'What?' snapped Fielding.

'That Picasso,' said Grossman. 'That Pablo.' He looked up at Fielding. 'I lent him a pencil once, you know. He was short a pencil.' Grosssman, still chuckling, shook his head. 'That wily Spanish bastard. He never gave it back.'

Fielding, despite himself, blinked.

'Yeah?' he said.

'That's right,' Grossman said. 'I remember the scene. I remember exactly. It's as clear to me as a picture. We were sitting, a whole bunch. Braque was there, Picabia, Gris, a couple others, one or two dealers. Suddenly Picasso taps his pocket. The other pocket. Nothing there. "Listen," he says to me. "Gimme a pencil. Quick. No pencil, no Cubism!" '

Fielding blinked again.

'And you gave it to him?'

'Sure,' said Grossman. 'Of course. Why not?'

'Sucker!' Fielding howled.

And then laughed, rocking back on his high silver heels.

'You're a damn phoney, Grossman!' Fielding shouted. 'A hundred per cent damn phoney, you know that?'

Grossman shrugged, unharmed.

'Please yourself, Professor,' he said. 'Please yourself.'

'OK, OK,' Fielding hurried in. 'Don't get sore. You want to tell me about Paris? Go ahead, tell me about Paris. But speed it up, gramps, make it fast. I got a trillion better ways to spend my time than listen to this old shit.'

Grossman replaced his eyeglasses, readjusted the scarf, fussed with a button on his jacket.

'Oh, I see,' Fielding said. 'Now you're gonna go all coy. You're not going to tell me anything.'

'I was thinking,' Grossman said.

Fielding blew exasperated smoke.

'I'll bet,' he said.

'Fitzgerald,' Grossman said.

'F. Scott?' Fielding asked.

'That's him,' Grossman said. 'That's the one. A nice boy. A nice talent. Everything beautiful. Except. Well, he had a thing.'

'A what thing?' Fielding shot in.

'Well, a private thing,' Grossman hedged.

'Come on,' Fielding urged. 'Let's hear it.'

'Well,' said Grossman, looking down at his hands, 'he was unsure of himself, Fitzgerald, you'll excuse the language, with regard to the size of his, um, his *shlong*.'

'Oh, that!' Fielding sneered. 'Everyone knows that! It's in all the books. Jesus. Big deal. So what else is new?'

'I saw it,' Grossman whispered.

'What?' Fielding snapped. 'You personally saw F. Scott Fitzgerald's . . .?'

Grossman chuckled shyly.

'Of course,' he said, 'that's also not so unique. Everyone saw it. Ho, that Fitzgerald. Everywhere he went it was instantly out, showing here, showing there, excuse me, you don't think my *shlong* is inadequate, do you? I tell you, half the population of Paris used to carry a tape measure, it was the only way to reassure him he was all right.'

'Is that so?' Fielding said.

Grossman mused and rocked.

'Vell, an artist,' he said. 'A creative person. You know how they are, those people. Always seeking reassurance, no matter how big the talent.'

'Aw, bullcrap!' Fielding howled. 'Reassurance, my ass! Listen, I've got a little something going in the creative department myself, you think I'm all the time whipping out my *shlong*, getting opinions on size, like it was some friggin' *Gallup poll* or something?'

Grossman said nothing.

'Well, maybe three, four times,' Fielding admitted, shuffling his feet. 'But that was with friends, not total strangers! And certainly not with half the population of friggin' Paris!'

Grossman's shrug was minimal, noncommital.

'Listen,' said Fielding, his voice suddenly lower, confidential. 'This, uh, F. Scott's, um, his *thing* . . . was it . . .?'

Grossman carefully measured out a distance between upright hands.

'Yeah?' said Fielding, staring. 'Like that? Wow.'

Grossman pondered, added a further inch.

'Gee,' said Fielding. 'A thing like that and he went round all the time asking . . . Hey, listen, gramps!' Fielding's voice was suddenly up again. 'It ever occur to you that the great F. Scott was doin' something else? Like, *soliciting for a blowjob*!'

Grossman looked up, amazed.

'A fag, you mean?' he whispered, disbelieving.

'Yeah!' spat out Fielding. 'A ding dong fuggin' fag!'

'Hmmm,' mused Grossman, reaching for a ledger, a pen. 'Hmmm. That's a very deep psychological insight you've got there, Professor. Hmmm. Very astute.'

Grossman began to write quickly in the ledger.

'Wait a minute,' Fielding interrupted. 'What's that book? What are ya doin' in there?'

'Oh,' said Grossman, looking bashful. 'Vell, it's, uh, vell . . . my memoirs.'

'Your memoirs?'

'Vell, just a footnote to history,' Grossman allowed. 'You know, a few thoughts, a few experiences.'

He smiled modestly.

'You have to understand,' he said. 'For me it was really something. One minute in the Yeshiva, the next I'm in Gay Paree.'

Grossman closed the ledger, patted it affectionately.

'Don't worry, Professor,' he said. 'For that psychological insight I'll give you full credit. In things like that, I am not a *ganef*.'

'Yeah, I bet,' Fielding scowled. 'So, what else? Fitzgerald's *shlong*. Big deal. That's your whole book?'

'And the pencil to Picasso,' Grossman reminded him.

'So OK,' said Fielding. 'Two things. I still don't see a book.'

Grossman was for a long moment silent.

'Hemingway,' he said at last. 'We ran together with the bulls in Pamplona.'

'So?' said Fielding.

'Oh, he was a winner, that Poppa,' Grossman chuckled. 'Ho ho, what a boychick. Always had to be first.'

'So?' said Fielding. 'Come on, gramps. Spit it out. You got inside dope or not?'

'He wore rollerskates,' Grossman triumphantly announced.

'Sheeeet!' sung out Fielding.

'I saw it,' said Grossman. 'With my own eyes.'

Fielding shook his head, collected himself.

'OK,' he said. 'That's not bad. But it's not much either. Ya got anything else?'

'Henry Miller,' Grossman breathed.

'Is that so?' Fielding said.

'*The Tropic of Capricorn.*'

'And?'

'You will recall,' said Grossman, 'that section where a person named Curley is having a *shtupp* with a certain Valeska?'

Fielding nodded impatiently.

'How he liked to make with her the wheelbarrow, or the dog fashion?'

Fielding nodded faster.

'Yeah, yeah. So?'

'And then finally one day with the back-scuttle, how he suddenly pulled out the *shlong* and popped in instead a carrot?'

'Yeah, yeah. Well?'

Grossman smiled up like a satisfied cat.

'I supplied the vegetable.'

Fielding stepped back, speechless.

'Oh those Paris days,' Grossman mused softly, rocking in memory, lost in recollection, his moans and sighs faint in the tumult of the close-at-hand, raucous jazz still booming.

And then suddenly he looked up at Fielding again.

'Oh, but I haven't told you the best thing,' he said. 'The top moment of my whole French experience!'

Fielding waited, tensed.

'I once sat,' Grossman confided proudly, 'on Gertrude's lap.'

'What?' said Fielding, awed at last. 'Gertrude *Stein*?'

Grossman chuckled softly.

'Alice never forgave me,' he said. 'I tried to explain it to her. I told her I thought it was an armchair. Whooo. She got so annoyed. You've never seen such annoyed. When she served the chocolate cake, she gave me only a child's portion.'

'Wow,' said Fielding. 'And how was it? I mean, the lap?'

Grossman seemed to become smaller, to shrink back in time, burrowed deep in memory.

'Vast,' he whispered finally. 'Vast.'

Fielding stared at him, lost for words, and then suddenly snapped open his shoulderbag, fed himself a fresh piece of gum, and then bent over Grossman, the Fielding of before, brash and glossy, brooking no crap.

'OK, gramps,' he said. 'Memory time is over, finito, no more. Very interesting, I'm sure, not that I believed a fuggin' word of it. The closest you ever got to France, Grossman, was the mustard! Haw haw!' Then Fielding's face snapping back to ice. 'OK. Enough horsin' around. Let's have the bread.'

Grossman stood slowly, shuffled to his desk, drew open a drawer, Fielding crowded behind, boogying to the music, sashaying and swinging, fingers popping, the Afro in tumult, but watching Grossman lynx-eyed.

'And none of that short change shit either,' Fielding snapped.

Grossman counted out money with thick, clumsy fingers.

Fielding grabbed, riffed it quickly, crammed it into the shoulderbag out of sight.

'OK, gramps,' he said, snatching another fifty out of Grossman's hand. 'Like, later.'

Grossman hobbled to open the door.

'Hey, that's some music you've got there, gramps,' Fielding said, boogying and swinging, his mood restored with the money in his bag. 'What's the station? I might check it out on my radio when I get back to the hotel.'

'Radio?' said Grossman, blinking. 'There is no radio. I have no radio.'

And he whisked back a black curtain, revealing in the space behind the classic bop quintet, two horns and rhythm section, the drummer slapping, the bass player pounding, the pianist dropping in meaty chords, the tenor player buzzing on the sidelines, and out in front the trumpeter taking his solo, hunched forward in an S-shape, mute tight to the mike, burning his way through *Bye Bye Blackbird*, and then swinging straight into *All Blues*.

Fielding stared, agape.

'Is that . . . *Miles Davis*?' he finally managed.

Grossman flew the curtain quickly back into place.

'Drop by Tuesdays,' Grossman smiled, the gold tooth jumping out in an insolent flash. 'I got me the Amadeus String Quartet.'

boss shes back i refer
of course to mrs
kinkaid the randy cleaning
lady you know boss
the one who did all those
juicy things
in the chiefs office
when she found the
tequila sorry i
didnt finish the tale
that time believe me i tried
but boss
sometimes even a humble cock

roach gets excited too
and i cant tell you the frazzle
i wore myself into
jumping on the typewriter keys
with not quite
all my legs
because i needed a few for other
purposes

well boss she starts right in
on the floors on her
hands and knees
look at those powerful arms
those wonderful legs
shes in a real sweat those
gorgeous hot slavic features all shiny
her thin cotton blouse
practically sopping
i have told you
boss havent i that she never
wears a bra
or pants either for that matter
under her short black skirt
and i am scurrying so fast
trying to decide
what to look at most
but oh boss i tell you
when god made perfection he really
outdid himself
with the working class
tush

boss i am running my legs off
you have no possible notion
of my speed
and just when i finally decide
its the tush for me
mrs kinkaid suddenly finds
her flopping about sweat drenched
thin cotton blouse
such a hindrance to her
movements so what the hell
off it flies through the
air like a jungle parrot coming
to rest on the back of
a chair and oh boss
they are so much bigger
than i ever dreamed
gently swinging and swaying
as she scrubs
like the bells of
cockroach heaven

ah but boss now shes
finished the floors and
she stands up
leaving her blouse right
where it is and
what a wonderful sweat
shes in rivulets
running front and back
and those jangly bangles
she wears
the little gold love chain

on her right ankle
that fierce black forest
of untamed hair
boss shes an amazonian princess
no less and now shes
going into the chiefs office
which is where she
did all that juicy stuff
last time

oh yes boss she remembers
look how shes fondling
the telephone
with her long fingers
in that special way she has
and the handle
on the bottom drawer where
the chief keeps the tequila and
whoops one of her hands
has disappeared
i mean its gone under her skirt
in the front and making those sounds
like truck tyres on a rainy road
oh this is one juicy lady
and her mouth has fallen open
and her eyes are going
all goofy
and boss now her other hand is
reaching for the feather duster
help i am falling
off the wall

Holy shit, late again!

'Sorry, sir. Alarm clock didn't go off, sir. Won't happen again, sir.'

Flushed, breathless Fielding, in tunic and blazer, boardingschool blue, white blouse somewhat grubby, white long socks, the lace untied and trailing on one scuffed black shoe, deposited quickly his essay and a shiny red apple on Grossman's table, retreated then to his desk in front, satchel clattering, hastily sat down.

Stern Grossman stared.

'What?' he finally erupted. '*Slept in?*'

'Yes, sir,' Fielding contritely whispered.

'Playing with yourself, were you, Fielding?'

'No, sir!'

'Hmmm?'

'No! Sir!'

'Teasing your little dickie bird under the blankets, hmmm?'

'No, sir! Never!'

'Having a little Jane Fonda fantasy, were we, hmmm? Charlie's Angels? Raquel Welch?'

'Sir!'

'A little bit of nookie pookie, what?'

Fielding dared outraged eyes.

'Bad for the skin, Fielding. Bad for the eyesight. Hair on the palms.'

Fielding quickly looked.

'Aha!'

Grossman there in a trice, swooping like a raven in his black academic gown, cuffing curtly the back of Fielding's head, a stinging edge-of-hand blow.

'Dirty boy!' thundered Grossman. 'Filthy little bugger!'

Fielding silent, head bowed, cheeks ablaze, brimming tears.

But Grossman unsatisfied, standing there still, arm drawn back as though to administer another blow.

'What are you, Fielding?' he demanded. 'Hmmm?'

'A dirty boy,' Fielding whispered.

'Speak up!' Grossman shouted, the arm trembling on the edge of movement. 'What else?'

'A ... a ... a ... filthy little bugger,' Fielding managed at last, his voice breaking, drowning in sobs.

'Humph!' grunted Grossman, drawing himself up, righteously erect.

And adjusting his mortarboard, flicking back the swinging tassel, straightening his black gown in front to hide away the disgusting stains beneath, he swept grandly back to his previous position, to the side of the blackboard, behind his table.

'Pusillanimous prick,' Fielding quietly mocked.

Grossman wheeled at once, alert as a hound.

'What was that, Fielding?'

'Nothing, sir!'

Grossman stared.

Fielding blinked innocent eyes.

'Hmmm,' Grossman growled.

But at last turned, reached for chalk, moved to the blackboard.

'Dropsied droop,' Fielding muttered.

But Grossman heard nothing.

Grossman was engaged.

Grossman, on the blackboard, expertly drew.

Leaving unobserved Fielding to fiddle quickly through the fabric of his tunic.

Cheekily tweaking.

Naughtily nudging.

In time to a Charlie's Angel slowly unrobing in the secret chamber of his hot mind.

And whoops just in time both hands up and away and plainly visible on the desk as Grossman spun suddenly around.

'Now!' snapped Grossman.

Fielding sat straight, chin up, keen eyes shining: a model student.

'Now!' said Grossman again, tapping the blackboard with his chalk. 'What have we here?'

'Um,' Fielding began, blinking hard, brow creased with effort.

'Speak up, boy!' Grossman volleyed.

'Um, the male member, sir?' Fielding attempted, taking a stab.

'The what?'

'Um ... the glans penis, sir?' Fielding tried again.

'Fielding!' Grossman was a thundercloud. 'Come on!'

'Um . . . the *shlong*, sir?' Fielding ventured, going for broke, face and hands in an absolute sweat.

'Good boy!' cried Grossman, applauding with a clap. 'Exactly! The *shlong*!'

Fielding pridefully glowed.

'Now,' said Grossman, pressing on. 'This *shlong*. What is it doing?'

'Um . . .' Fielding blinked again, feeling lost and foolish. 'Um, nothing, sir,' he said at last.

'Exactly!' cried Grossman, this time with a smile. 'Exactly! It's doing nothing! It's just hanging there! Like a dead banana! Limp and useless! Ha ha!'

And again he clapped his hands, chalkdust rising in a cloud.

'And what does it want to do, Fielding?'

'It wants to . . . it wants to . . .' Fielding stammered.

'Bah!'

His patience exhausted, Grossman spun back to the blackboard, his diagram this time rapid, the chalk flying in fierce angry strokes.

And then whirled back to face Fielding.

'It wants to do this!' Grossman shouted, pounding the blackboard with a heavy fist.

'Yes, sir!' Fielding responded.

'It wants to stand up!'

'Yes, sir!' Fielding cried again.

'But it can't do it alone, can it, Fielding?'

'No, sir!'

'It needs some encouragement!'

'Yes, sir!'

'It needs some help!'

'Yes, sir!'

'And how can we give it that encouragement, Fielding, how can we give it that help? Short of visiting it upon some tupenny whore with the risk – more than the risk! practically the certainty! – of attendant dreadful disease!'

Fielding looked nervously down at his desk.

'Well, Fielding?' Grossman demanded. 'Hmmm?'

Fielding felt again the welling of tears.

'I don't know, sir,' he mumbled.

'Don't know?' shouted Grossman. 'Don't know? Of course you know, boy! Think!'

'Masturbation, sir?' Fielding attempted.

'Feh!' exploded Grossman. 'Feh!'

And with a heavy sigh, Grossman sat down at his table, deflated, defeated.

'I don't know,' he said. 'I don't know. I teach, I explain, I make diagrams, I set tests. And for what? Nothing! In one ear and out the other. It's like pouring water onto desert sand.'

Foolish Fielding sunk deeper into his seat, his eyes cast down with shame.

The room ticked thickly with awkward silence.

'All right,' said Grossman finally. 'All right.' He stood up again, took a long breath, set his gown straight over his shoulders, tugged it in front for the folds to fall properly correct. He nodded. He creased his brow. He pursed his lips. He thought.

And then, summoning up a patient smile, calm at last, long-suffering Grossman began again.

'To create in the *shlong* a desire to become erect,' he lectured, 'we read to it a certain kind of prose. This prose we call by the name of pornography. Pornography,' he repeated. 'From the Greek *porne*, a harlot.'

Grossman looked suddenly up.

'Lummox!' he shouted. 'Swinebrain! Thickhead! Dolt! Oaf! Why are you not writing this down, Fielding? Why are you not taking notes? Do you think I am saying all this for my own amusement?'

'Yes, sir! No, sir!' Fielding shot back, in total confusion, bending to his satchel, grabbing books, pencils scattering, rolling all over the floor.

'Sorry, sir!'

Red-faced Fielding studiously wrote.

'The type of prose we are discussing here,' Grossman continued, his head nodding in time with the drone of his lecturing tone, 'is frequently classified as erotic, an adjectival word similarly derived from the Greek, this time *eros*, their word for love. But ah!' said Grossman, holding up a cautionary finger. 'What a difference we have here! What a chasm has opened between these two words!'

Fielding scribbled madly.

And then looked quickly up, ready for more.

But Grossman was gone, lost in some private world, deep in humming thought, a million miles away.

Fielding waited.

There seemed to be some activity taking place under Grossman's academic gown, a scuffling there, like a rat under a sheet.

Fielding smirked knowingly.

'Blowhole,' he whispered.

Grossman snapped awake, his guilty gape quickly covered by an equally guilty smile, and then the hand remembered and quickly reappeared, into the innocent open, the rodent flushed out.

'Oh, yes,' he said. 'Oh, yes. Hmmm. Where was I? Oh, yes. The function of pornography.'

Grossman began to pace, holding magisterially with both hands the lapels of his flowing gown.

'All life is a dream,' he intoned, 'spent in a minute, gone in the flash of an eye. An endless dream of the golden past. You doubt this? You speak of the present, the future? Hmmm? So. Let us consider, then, first the nature of this future, which we will define as that which has not yet come to pass. No? So. We strive, we plan, we envisage, we hope. We arrange, in those most secret compartments of our hearts and minds, the future of our most cherished desires.'

Fielding looked up, ready with a 'Yes, sir!' but none seemed required.

Grossman was in full flow.

Fielding quickly checked through his tunic the state of his pazzoo.

'We dream of a maiden with white thighs spread,' continued Grossman, pacing. 'We will have our way with her. We will plunge. She will moan. She will rake with her long nails the flesh of our back. She will snap and nip with pearly teeth in bites of love. Her breasts will bounce before us, cherry-topped pillows of hot creamy desire. Her legs will enfold us, drawing us ever closer, ever tighter. She will seize our tush, and we hers. Her long hair flying. Her legs like a vice. Hmmm?'

'Hot shit!' breathed Fielding, tweaking diabolically.

'But you will ask,' Grossman said, Fielding's activity unnoticed, his own sneakily resumed, 'what if it is the first time? What if we've never done it before? What if we live with the parents' bedroom door always locked and you can't even peep in the keyhole? And no older sisters either. So. From whence, then, comes this dream of the maiden?'

Fielding's mouth opened to speak.

Grossman quickly stilled him with an upraised finger.

'I will tell you,' he said. 'It is in our subconscious, the memory of the primeval *shtupp*! The mother! The father! And before them, the grandparents, the *bobbeh* and the *zaydeh* humping in their Polish *shtetl*! And each with his or her primeval *shtupp* buried deep in his or her primeval subconscious, buried there as deeply as we wish to bury ourselves in that maiden with white thighs spread not yet seen, never mind introduced, whom we envisage in what we call the future.'

'Jumping jism!' whispered Fielding, his hand a blur.

'And is there a present?' Grossman rhetorically enquired. And for answer, shook his head, sagely and slowly. 'No,' he said. 'The present is dwelt in dreams of the future. And the future, as I have shown, is nought but the selected remembrance of the golden past.'

Grossman smiled.

'Thus,' he said, 'the function and nature of pornography. To open those chambers of the subconscious, to ease the way for the jubilant *shlong*, to bring it forth, unashamed and proudly erect. In short, a service for mankind!'

'Oh, Jane!' panted hot-handed Fielding. 'Oh, Charlie's Angels! Oh, Raquel melon-breasted Welch!'

'Which is not to say there are not detractors,' snapped Grossman, his face suddenly surly. 'Oh, yes. There are those. The gossips. The forked tongues. The knives in the back. Pornography, they sneer. It incites, they proclaim. It inflames, they cry. It unbalances and unhinges, they wail and shout. It makes a hitherto meek and genteel insurance filing clerk suddenly leap out from behind a bush and pounce upon and have his dastardly way with some virginal female dental technician, a young and innocent girl only halfway through her lunch. To which I say: Fooey! Feh! Double feh! A total crock of shit! And do you know why I say this? Hmmm? Because, that young and innocent and so-called virginal female dental technician, ho ho, with those cute white stockings, with those sexy white flat-heeled little shoesies, with that crisp white short tiny little smock that doesn't even hardly cover her wonderfully juicy jutting tush, ho ho, now don't tell me she doesn't know what she's doing with all that, don't tell me she doesn't know with every little slightest bend you can't look straight up into that gorgeous little *hot box*!'

Grossman panted for breath.

Fielding the same.

Grossman, with an effort, calmed first.

'Well, Fielding, my lad,' he said, strolling to his desk, patting him affectionately on the top of his head, the fingers lingering there a little longer than was strictly necessary. 'You've been a good boy today. Very attentive. Thank you. Now, I will sit down and read your essay, and while I am doing that ... hmmm ...' Grossman stroked his chin, instantly deep in thought. 'Ah, yes,' he said. 'I have it. A small exercise. Let me see. Wheelchairs, wooden legs, plasma bags. In short, fiendish difficulties. But eros triumphant. Arouse me, Fielding, arouse me!'

A final fingering of Fielding's locks and Grossman marched back to his table.

Fielding took up his pen.

'Oh, and Fielding?' Grossman suddenly remembered.

Fielding looked expectantly up.

'Keep it crisp!'

'Yes, sir!' Fielding cried.

Grossman now sat and read, Fielding's essay this time aping the great Don Marquis, newspaperman, poet and drunk, who, in his creation of Archy the literary cockroach who flung his tiny body about on a typewriter to tell of the doings of Mehitabel. the cat, brought to the masses a thinly-disguised love of voyeurism and pussy.

Grossman read.

Fielding sat and wrote.

Ten minutes ticked by.

Fifteen.

Twenty.

Fielding, finished, bored and listless, began to inscribe into his desk top with the point of his compass the legend TEECHER IS A RANCID TERD.

And was rubbing it with spit to make it look ancient, the handiwork of some errant pupil long gone, when again the back of his head exploded with a crash.

'Out the front!' screeched Grossman. 'Out the front!'

Pushing him in the back to make him move faster.

'Filthy little bugger!' shouted Grossman, Fielding pushed now to the edge of his table. 'Up with the tunic!'

Red-faced Fielding did as bid.

'And the bloomers!' Grossman cried.

'But, sir . . .' Fielding attempted.

'Right down!' Grossman howled. 'To the ankles!'

Fielding bent, as he had done so many times before.

'Cup the cods!' snapped Grossman.

Fielding closed his eyes.

'Vun!' shouted Grossman, bringing down the cane.

The pain was unspeakable.

Fielding gasped.

'Two!'

Fielding silently howled.

'Three!'

Tears jumped from Fielding's eyes.

'Four!'

Fielding fought to still his cry.

'Five!'

Fielding was on fire.

'Six!'

Fielding fell forward, collapsed in a heap.

'All right,' said Grossman, breathing stentoriously, a booming soundtrack. 'Let that be a lesson.'

Fielding bent to draw up his bloomers, turned away from Grossman to hide his boner, Grossman similarly turned away, something fierce of his own savagely distorting the fall of his black academic gown.

Fielding hobbled back to his seat.

'All right,' said Grossman. 'All right. Where was I? Oh, yes. Fielding? Come forward. Take your essay.'

Again Fielding hobbled out, eyes down, to Grossman's table.

To see, with falling heart, that Grossman had marked him a mere C+.

'I took marks off for lack of neatness,' Grossman said. 'I don't like sloppy work.'

'Yes, sir,' Fielding said.

'Smudges,' said Grossman.

'Yes, sir.'

'Blots.'

'Yes, sir.'

'Stains in the margins of the most disgusting and suspicious nature.'

'Yes, sir,' said Fielding, standing before Grossman, head bowed, eyes lowered too. 'It won't happen again, sir.'

'I trust not,' said Grossman. 'Well,' he said, consulting his watch. 'I see our time is once again up.'

'Yes, sir,' said Fielding.

'Until next week.'

'Yes, sir.'

'All right, Fielding,' said Grossman. 'You may go.'

'Thank you, sir,' said Fielding. 'Good afternoon, sir.'

And grabbing his satchel Fielding was almost out the door, his brain whirling with the twin plan of getting his pazzoo into Jane Fonda, Raquel Welch and all the Charlie's Angels in the one steamy fantasy and showing what he could really do with an essay that would win at least a B, when Grossman spoke again.

'Oh, Fielding?'

Fielding turned, an insect pinned to a board.

But Grossman was smiling, holding aloft the shiny red fruit.

'Tenks for de apple.'

<u>Who's Afraid of Sigmund Freud?</u>

If you really want to hear about it, the first thing you'll probably want to know is how I finally lost my virginity and all, and did she have big knockers or just those dreadful falsies that stick out all over the place, and what we did exactly, and all that Harold Robbins kind of crap. I mean, did we do it normal, like just sitting on each other's face with cold-pressed vegetable oil and all that, or really perverted, like the stuff I was watching out my goddam hotel window while I was waiting for this girl – this prostitute, *for God's sake – to arrive.*

I'd lined it all up with the elevator operator, this guy named Neville. Neville. *That really kills me.*

'Innarested in a little tail t'night, chief?' he'd asked me, the minute I stepped into his crumby elevator.

'No, thanks,' I'd said, 'but I sure could use a girl.'

Boy, did I think I was witty. Grinning like crazy, too. Sometimes I swear to God I'm a madman.

Anyhow, there I was up in my goddam hotel room, waiting for the prostitute and trying to decide whether to wear my old red hunting hat or not – I've got this great old red hunting hat which I've had for about a million years – and looking out the window at the rooms on the other side. The place was crawling with perverts. They didn't even bother to pull their shades down. I saw one guy, a pretty old guy but still handsome, if you know what I mean, take off all his clothes, including his shorts, and then he did something you wouldn't believe me if I told you. First he put his suitcase on the bed. Then he took out this crazy octopus suit and put it on – a huge octopus suit, tentacles and all. I swear to God. Then, when he had it on, he climbed up on top of his closet and just sat there, not doing anything special, except every now and then just giving his tentacles a kind of a shake. There must have been about seventy of them, for God's sake, sort of hanging over the edge of the goddam closet. I don't know if he was saying anything, or making any kind of special octopus sound, but I don't think he was. I mean, I couldn't hear him or anything, of course, what with the space between us and the closed windows, his and mine, but it certainly didn't look like that was what he was doing. He did it for hours, the sitting up there, I mean, shaking his tentacles. And then all of a sudden this big fish swam into the room – it must have been in the bathroom all the time, I guess. She – the fish, I mean, but you could tell it was a woman, on account of the terrific legs – was sort of wriggling along on the carpet, coming closer and closer to the closet. And then the octopus must have seen her, because all of a sudden his tentacles went all stiff. But I didn't really see what happened after that because just then there was this knock on the door and I got such a surprise I dropped my goddam telescope.

When I opened the door, this nun was standing there. She had on one of those black habits that nuns wear, and those glasses with iron rims that aren't too attractive. And she had one of those straw baskets that you see nuns and Salvation Army babes collecting dough with around Christmas time. 'Sorry,' I said, 'I gave at the office.' Suave as hell, boy. I mean, I didn't even have an office.

'Aw, cut the crap,' she said. 'You the guy Neville said?'

'Is he the elevator boy?'

'Yeah,' she said.

'Allow me to introduce myself. My name is J. D. Tungsten-Steel,' I said.

'Yeah?' she said. Then, what she did, she reached over and tweaked my wuddayacallit. She gave it a hell of a tweak, if you'd really like to know. It just about made my old red hunting hat jump off my head. Actually, my old red hunting hat was the other thing I was wearing. Except, of course, for my socks.

'Would you care for a cigarette?' I said.

'I don't smoke,' she said. Then she sat down on my goddam lap. 'You're cute.'

Then she started getting funny. Crude and all. She

gave me this terrifically dirty look. It was really quite embarrassing. It really was. I mean, she was still in her nun's habit and all, and I was standing up, and she hadn't even come into the goddam room yet.

'Hey, you a virgin *or something?' she said.*

'I was,' I said, 'just before you sat on my goddam lap. But don't let that stop ya.' God, I wish you could've been there. She was a real prince.

'It all began,' Fielding began, 'that night I opened the door of my parents' bedroom. I was three years old.'

Fielding on the couch.

Grossman on a chair.

The sounds of their breathing.

Otherwise, silence.

'Yass?' said Grossman, finally.

Fielding stirred.

'I don't know why I did it,' he continued. 'I mean, usually I slept the whole night through. Never got up. Not for anything. Wouldn't dream of interrupting my parents.'

'*Dream?*' said Grossman, leaning closer.

Fielding suddenly chuckled.

'Well, plus the fact that I was always tied up,'

he explained. 'Hand and foot, actually. Damned tight, too. So this particular night, let me see . . . Oh, yes! The steak knife! My nanny had smuggled a steak knife in, with which I managed to sever my bonds.'

'A nanny?' prompted Grossman. 'Hmmm?'

'Why, yes,' Fielding said. 'Miss Gonads. A Spanish girl. Quite pretty, too. If you discounted the moustache. Oh, and her armpits – those jutting black nests. How unruly they were! Positively *leapt* at you every time she reached over to ladle out the porridge.'

'Ho, ho, those Spanish ladies,' chortled Grossman. 'Well do I know them. Those bawds of Malaga, those strumpets of Seville, those red-hot randy whores of Madrid.'

'What?' said Fielding, confused and blinking. He started to sit up. 'But Miss Gonads was from Barcelona . . .'

'No, no,' said Grossman, restraining Fielding with a professional hand. 'Merely a private rumination, an errant thought. Pray continue.'

Fielding again prone, blinking and thinking.

And then suddenly a cry.

'Wait a minute, Doc! Wait a minute! It's coming back to me! Yes! That night . . . for the first time ever . . . I had a wet dream! I dreamt . . . yes, yes . . . I dreamt I was milking Sparky!'

'Sparky?' said Grossman. 'What is this Sparky? You had by you a *cow*?'

'What?' cried Fielding. 'How dare you! I was never into cows! Jesus! What do you think I am, some kind of pimple-ravaged perverted barnyard *creep*? Shit, Doc. Sparky was my collie. My dog. My faithful four-legged *friend*!'

Fielding breathed deeply, exhaled with passion, a censorious sound.

'Every boy should have a dog,' he said sternly. 'Instils a sense of responsibility. Develops the character. Best thing in the world.'

Fielding turned suddenly to regard Grossman.

'Hey, you Jews never have dogs, do you?' Fielding's voice was accusatory and thin. 'Why is that, I wonder? Hey, Jewboy, what's with the no dogs? Ya too mean to feed 'em, is that it? Hey, Jewboy? Come on, Fagin, speak up there. Ya begrudge 'em a little bone? Hello, Sparky!' Fielding suddenly called, his voice flying up to an adolescent soprano, his hands springing to his chest to hang bent-wristed, a flawless imitation of his fawning pet. 'Have a nice day, Sparky? Chase a lot of pussy cats? Woof woof! Bow wow!'

'Fielding!' snapped Grossman, slapping down the hands. 'Control yourself! Please!'

'Oops, sorry, Doc.' Fielding collected himself quickly. 'Must have got carried away. Where was I?'

Grossman consulted his notebook.

'The dog, the milking,' he read out.

'Oh, yeah,' Fielding said. 'Right. Well. The next thing I knew, I was drenched. I mean, absolutely sopping. You've got no idea. On my rubber sheet, too. Wow, that was something. I didn't know what had happened. I thought I'd sprung a leak in there or something, ha ha.'

'So then you cut your bonds?'

'Well, not straight away,' Fielding explained. 'First I had a little bit of an exploratory wank. Just to see if I was still firing.'

'And were you?'

'Doctor!' said Fielding. 'Please. If you don't mind. Some things are just too personal to discuss.'

'Whoosh, I am so sorry, Mr Fielding,' said Grossman quickly. 'Pardon me. I meant no disrespect.'

'Right,' said Fielding, his voice properly gruff. 'Long as that's clear. Now let me see. Oh, yeah. The wet dream, the rubber sheet, the supplementary wank. Did I forget anything?'

'The nanny?' Grossman asked hopefully.

'Oh, Jesus, Doc!' Fielding exploded. 'You and that friggin' nanny! Can't you think of anything else? Anyhow, my nanny had nothing to do with it. My nanny was under the bed.'

'Under the bed?' said Grossman incredulously. 'Under the bed? This whole time your nanny was there under the bed?'

'Shit, Doc,' Fielding whined. 'Don't you understand *anything*?' He took and exhaled a deep exasperated breath. 'She was *always* there. That was her *place*!'

'I see, I see,' said Grossman, scribbling rapidly in his notebook. 'Yes, yes, the picture is quite clear now. Forgive me.'

'OK,' said Fielding slowly. 'So then I cut the bonds. So then I went to my parents' bedroom. So then I opened the door. So then I looked in at what was happening in there. And remember, all this time I was still only three years old.'

'Absolutely,' said Grossman, setting alight a huge Havana.

'Yeah,' said Fielding. 'And don't you forget it. Three golden years old. An angelic babe in arms. A mite. A tot. A tiny handful of milk-pure innocence. A faint ray of sunshine in a dirty wicked world.'

Grossman withheld comment.

'So in I go,' continued Fielding. 'And what do I see? My parents. My progenitors. My beloved mother and father. Momsy and pops. The pair of them, prancing around the room. Dressed up like a common sailor and dowager Duchess.'

'Your daddy in a sailor suit?' said Grossman, eyes flaring, leaning forward.

'No, no,' Fielding quickly corrected him. 'My *mother* was the sailor. My dear old dad was the dowager Duchess.'

'I see,' said Grossman, drawing on his cigar.

'You don't see nothin', Doc,' Fielding snapped. 'Because I haven't even told you yet that my father sported a magnificent salt and pepper full chest-length beard, which was more than slightly at odds, I can assure you, with his dowager Duchess ensemble.'

'And your mother?' Grossman enquired.

'Likewise, likewise,' said Fielding. 'A similarly jarring note. Lipstick, rouge, earrings, necklace. Momsy was one cute sailor boy, believe you me.'

'Hmmmm,' mused Grossman, twirling his cigar. 'A little role reversal. Hmmmm. A little prancing. Hmmmm. And then a nice *shtupp*.'

'What?' Fielding cried. 'Get outta here, Doc! This is my mother and father you're talking about, my dear momsy and pops! Jeez!'

Grossman quickly stammered an apology.

Fielding righteously sniffed.

'OK,' continued Fielding, when he was good and ready. 'Now I'll tell you what happened. After the prancing, which went on for some considerable time, round the room, over the bed, all over the place, me standing there in the doorway during it all completely and totally unnoticed and unremarked, and still only a mere three years old, momsy and pops suddenly ducked behind this screen they had in there, over by the far wall. Whoops, they were gone. Completely out of sight. I couldn't see a thing. But I could hear. First there was huffing, and then there was puffing, and then all these zippers going zip, and then the shoes too, clomp clomp, and suddenly there was the sailor suit, and the dowager Duchess ensemble, recklessly strewn all over the floor.

'Preparatory to *shtupping*?' Grossman whipped in.

'Get outta here, Doc!' Fielding howled. 'What's the matter with you? Jeez. I don't know. Listen, that's some kind of diseased mind you've got there, you know that? You should have it looked at some time. No, I mean that. Seriously. No kidding.'

'I'm sorry,' Grossman whimpered. 'Really, I'm very sorry, Mr Fielding. Truly I am. It won't happen again. I promise. Cross my heart.'

'Well, OK,' Fielding said. 'Just this once. But

watch it, right? Enough is enough. OK. The sailor. The Duchess. Behind the screen. The huffing, the puffing, the zips, the shoes. And then all of a sudden out they come again.'

'Naked?' cried Grossman, with a salacious slap of his hands. 'Buck-naked?'

'Naked nothing!' Fielding cried. 'Deep sea scuba diver and World War One Luftwaffe Ace!'

'Mein Gott!' cried Grossman.

'You said it,' Fielding snapped. 'And I'm talking authentic! Every detail, perfect and correct. And I don't mean just mask and flippers, boots and cap – anyone can do that! I mean oxygen cylinders, spear gun, monocle, cork-tipped cigarette – the whole dang shooting match! Absolutely amazing. I don't know how they did it in the time.'

'And your father?' asked Grossman. 'Which one was he? The Luftwaffe Ace, I presume?'

'Wrong again, Doc, wrong again.' Fielding slowly shook his head. 'I don't think you understand *anything*. I'm beginning to wonder if you're even a qualified *doctor*. Scuba, man, scuba!' he shouted. 'Dad was the scuba diver! Got it now?'

'Oh, of course,' said Grossman quickly, hiding his confusion by scribbling rapidly in his pad. 'How stupid of me. Please accept my full apologies.'

'Yeah,' said Fielding. 'Dad was the deep sea scuba diver. Black rubber, head to toe. Plus the speargun. And his mask all filled up with his magnificent salt and pepper full chest-length beard. I tell you, it was like the Sargasso Sea in there. But it didn't seem to bother pops. Not for a minute. He was too busy, prancing around the room, his flippers going flap, flap, flap as he chased my Luftwaffe mom, with me still standing there in the doorway, mute observer, endlessly aged three.'

'And did he catch her?' Grossman asked, breath quickening. 'Catch her and bear her to the floor and strip from her body that Luftwaffe costume – oh what a pretty struggle! – and then himself likewise, out of that clinging head-to-toe foul black rubber suit, and then, and then, both of them entirely and completely buck-naked, throw into that area between her parted white welcoming but simultaneously resisting thighs a resounding and profoundly satisfying for both of them deep and noisy *shtupp*?'

Fielding sighed wearily, for extra measure throwing in a heaven-directed roll of the eyes.

'Doc,' he said, 'it was only half past two in the morning. All they'd done was the sailor and the Duchess, the scuba and the Luftwaffe Ace. They hadn't even *started* yet. They hadn't done the barber and the scullery maid, the gas man and the sword swallower, the librarian and the hunchback, the elephant and the King of Siam.'

A stunned Grossman shook his head.

'Whoosh!' he said. 'Whoosh! So many things!'

Slapping his cheeks incredulously, his eyes huge, his head shaking.

And then suddenly snapping back to business. Crossing his legs. Flipping to a fresh page on his notebook. Taking a long deep suck on his huge Havana.

'Very interesting, Mr Fielding,' he said at last. 'Very interesting, I'm sure. A classic case, if ever I saw one. Oh, yes. A real classic. But never mind the scuba, the Luftwaffe, the Duchess and all that. Red herrings. At last we come to the nub, the nexus. The elephant! Ho ho, the elephant, always the elephant. Featuring the basic symbolism, as I'm sure you've noticed, of the long trunk. Yes, indeedie! Here we are at last!'

Grossman gave to his cigar a positively lascivious suck.

'The charades and the masquerades and the prancing games are finally done,' he pronounced. 'The foreplay is over. Now he, your father, and she, your mother, fall at last content and happy into each other's waiting arms. At last, finally, as dawn is breaking gently in the sky, the crowing of cocks, the rattling of milk bottles, the drunken neighbours reeling wearily home from a night on the tiles, he and she, your father and mother, have themselves finally a fantastic galvanic volcanic –'

'Doctor!' Fielding screamed. 'Doctor! How many times do I have to tell you? No! No! A thousand times no.'

'No?' said Grossman.

'No.'

'They didn't *shtupp*?'

'When it was all over,' said Fielding, explaining it carefully as though speaking to a child, 'they tidied up all the clothes, put them all neatly away, and then my mother went off to sleep with the maid, the way she always did, under my bed, and my father went to *his* bed, the way *he* always did, with a wetted loaf of hollowed-out bread.'

Grossman sat speechless.

'Ah, memories,' Fielding quietly mused. 'Memories.'

Grossman stood up.

Fielding looked up.

Grossman, staring at the floor, hands clasped behind his back, began to pace.

Fielding sat up, blinking.

Grossman paced and paced, head down, cigar puffing.

'Well, Fielding,' he said at last. 'You've certainly opened up here a can of worms and no mistake.'

'I know it,' said Fielding quietly. 'Don't I know it.'

'The perversions,' said Grossman.

'Absolutely,' said Fielding.

'The grossness.'

'Exactly.'

'The filth.'

'Never a truer word.'

'And not only the perversions and the grossness and the filth,' intoned Grossman, resuming his pacing, the hands clasped as before, the cigar emitting regular puffs like an old-fashioned locomotive toiling up an incline, 'but all as witnessed by a mere mite of three years of age, and now forever

stamped with the scars and shadows of his parents'
sins, and doomed forever to be the envy of his likewise denied friends.'

'That's it exactly,' said Fielding, sitting with
bowed head. 'That's exactly it.'

Grossman came now to a stop before Fielding.

He looked gravely down.

And then the command, a curt nod of his chin.

Fielding fell to his knees on the floor, head still
bowed, but first quickly tucking up the hem of his
bright green crepe de chine cocktail frock.

Now Grossman, mumbling, made incantatory
signs and gestures over Fielding's bowed head.

'A handful Hail Marys,' he chanted, 'a couple
Ave Marias, two or three words The Lord's Prayer.
Hmmm. Hmmm. Yes, yes. Walk tall. Sleep
straight. Keep a clean nose. What else, what else
. . . Never wank unless you can think of something.
And . . . oh, yes . . . be careful, not too much salt
in the diet.'

Fielding on his knees stayed silent.

'Hokay,' said Grossman. 'I think that's about it.'

Grossman, nodding, turned, bent low.

'Kiss my ring.'

My Son the Pornographer

It was a dingy three-storey frame-house with a tattered grassplot out front and nothing special to mark it save for the flashing neon sign blinking on and off day and night without words but the picture of how it was done for the benefit of the illiterate white trash clientele.

'Miss Ruta Reena,' his pappy introduced him, and he looked up for the first time at that large woman in black silk and feathers holding up what at first he thought were two pink-nosed dogs, their wet snouts snivelling, but then he saw they maybe wasn't dogs, they were Miss Reena, a part of her, anyways.

'I brung the boy,' his pappy said.

And another dog he saw then, or what at first he

thought was a dog, a long-haired black animal with somehow pink lips through the hair showing wet, moiling about between Miss Reena's huge white thighs, where the black silk and the feathers didn't entirely reach over to ward off the chill.

'And I brung four kegs for payment,' his pappy said. And Miss Reena shouted.

'Gals,' she shouted. 'Git yore workin' parts down here. Pappy's brung his boy aged more than twelve to show him how it's done.'

And then the room where he stood side by side with his pappy filled up with ladies each one carrying what at first he thought were pink-nosed dogs and long-haired black ones moiling everywhere too, these easier to discern on them than on Miss Reena, she, Miss Reena, being the only one with black silk and feathers, the others all buck-naked oblivious to the chill except for the one who wore a gaudy flowered hat.

'Line up. Turn round. Spread your charms, gals,' Miss Reena said. 'Show pappy and the boy what they kin have.'

Then he saw his pappy taking a long time, squinting and sniffing and bending and inspecting, working harder even than when he was making purchase of new denims at the Grope's Landing General Store, the indecision mottling his face red and his tongue lolling, and finally settling on the lady in the gaudy flowered hat.

'What's yore name, honey?' he heard his pappy ask.

'Minnie,' she said.

And he saw her mouth open when she said it and the gap where three teeth had gone under the black mous-

tache and her huge white thighs run through with whorls like marbled lard and two smaller black dogs under her arms, one under each, dangling and jumping, from out of the pits.

'Pappy,' said Miss Reena. 'You always do choose the purtiest.'

And then the one called Minnie and his pappy went up the stairs with him following, and then into a room off the landing at the top where there was just a bed.

'Mount it, bawd,' his pappy said.

And up went Minnie in her gaudy flowered hat and nothing else, the shucks moving in the thin mattress, and when she was securely placed and lying flat on her back and opened and spread her huge white lard-whorled thighs he saw it weren't a mere dog she had in there moiling, it were a bear.

'Stand close, boy,' his pappy said to him, simultaneous to dropping off his denim work overall and standing entire buck-naked in the room, his corn-cob huge but flopping with a crab-apple perched on the end.

'Holp me up, boy,' his pappy said. 'I'm a mite sore from working that bottom forty.'

He helped his pappy up onto the bed, listening to the shucks moving in the thin mattress, raised him up to fit between the spread white lard thighs and his pappy coming to rest along the whole vast length of her and his mouth fixing itself on one of those pink-nosed dogs and straightaway setting up a guzzling the likes of which he'd only seen that time old Sam Grope's hog bust out of the pen and got into Mrs Farquarson's greens, that prissy schoolmarm, while Minnie just lay back with her *hands tucked away neat behind her gaudy flowered hat and looking up at the ceiling with profound disinterest and whistling softly between the gap in her teeth.*

'Now lean close, boy,' his pappy said to him then, speaking around the perky pink-nosed dog he seemed in no mind to stop guzzling. 'Lean in close and pay tight attention, boy. This is where I is gonna need your real holp.'

Exasperated with shaving, his shins a mess, Fielding plunged for woolly leg-warmers, raspberry and pistaccio in alternating luscious lollipop bands, followed up with hot pants in sassy satin peach, a silky zip-up baseball jacket and matching peaked cap, completing the ensemble with high-heeled pink sneakers tied with floppy white bows.

Oh cutie-pie Fielding.

Teeny bopper.

Jail bait.

A pervert's dream.

And with a wave and a wink to Miss Barthelmess, oh so fresh and clean and pink and shiny and virginal and innocent at her tidy desk, he sauntered in, flipping the door to behind him with an arrogant slam, one hand on a hip, from the other an expertly nonchalant yo-yo whipping through Walkin' the Dog, Around the World, Rockin' the Baby in its Cradle.

'Hi, Pops!' Fielding sang. 'Hey, listen, let me have –'

Grossman's voice was a black knife.

'Be quiet! What's the matter with you! Can't you see I'm *reading*?'

Fielding's sassiness fled like smoke.

'Oh . . . sorry . . .' he stammered. 'I didn't . . .'

Grossman ignored him.

Spurned him completely.

Didn't even look up.

He sat, Grossman, dour and sour, dumpy and lumpy, suspenders dangling, trouser-bottoms clumsily rolled, his eyeglassed eyes moving over the newspaper he gripped with fists an inch from his face, steam rising in the wan light from the tin tub in which he soaked his aged feet.

Sternly, he read.

Grunting.

Growling.

Turning, suddenly, a page, his fists fighting the newspaper as though in a wind, smiting, punching, flattening the battered sheets with impatient, furious slaps.

'Shit!' seethed Fielding. 'What a pig! How is anyone supposed to read the paper after he's done that to it? Good God almighty, who does he think he is, the only person in the world?'

Grossman shot without apology a dreadful fart.

Fielding closed embarrassed eyes.

Endless minutes ticked.

'Um, Pop . . .?' Fielding finally ventured, his face prepared with a winsome beseeching smile.

Grossman's eyes flicked up.

Murderous as poison.

'Did you wipe your feet?'

'Well . . . no . . . I . . .'

'Dolt! Idiot! How many times do I have to tell you?'

'Sorry . . .' Fielding stammered, retreating backwards, frantically wiping.

'Blockhead!' Grossman gave him for reward. 'Filth! Manure! Carrier of cholera!'

A note fell from Fielding's pocket.

'Vot's dat?' Grossman pounced.

'Oh . . .' Fielding blundered awkwardly, blood rushing to his face. 'It's just . . .'

'Give it here!'

Grossman snatched from Fielding's hand, brought it to his eyes, squinted, stared, his thick lips moving as he read the words.

Fielding, on fire, shuffled from foot to foot.

'A Father and Son Night,' Grossman arduously read. His eyes swung up. 'Vot's dis? Uh?'

'Well . . .' Fielding began, nervously scratching his cheek. 'You see . . .'

Grossman's eyes dived back to the note.

'A doctor will be in attendance,' he read. His face shot up again. 'What? What doctor?'

Fielding's hands didn't know what to do.

'Uh?' Grossman demanded. 'Fool! Speak up!'

'Well . . .' Fielding finally managed. 'It's . . . it's a kind of . . .'

Grossman whipped his eyes from Fielding's discomfort, shuddering in distaste.

'Feh!' he spat.

And plunged back to the note.

'Aha!' he cried.

He nodded his head.

'So!'

He stroked his chin.

'Sexual education,' he read slowly.

His eyebrows rose.

'An illustrated talk with slides and diagrams to explain the mysteries of life.'

Grossman smacked his lips.

'Dr Phineas Neugeboren, the esteemed authority and specialist,' he read, 'will be in personal attendance to answer any questions you may wish to have, following which a supper will be served.'

Grossman looked now wholly up at mortified Fielding.

His thick liverish lips moving to form a slow, mocking smile.

'The froggies, uh?' he said. 'The rabbits? The bees and the birds and the little pretty flowers?'

Fielding stood redder than a beet.

'Whoo whoo!' cried Grossman. '*Shtupping*!'

Fielding wanted to die.

Now Grossman was brisk, brusque.

'You don't need it!

'Nah!

'What for?

'Foreplay? Backplay?

'All that fancy shit?

'Feh!

'Listen, you stick it in, that's the whole business.

'You don't need doctors to tell you that.

'What?

'Diseases?

'You're worried with diseases?

'Give it a wash!

'All right, before and after, you want to be so fussy.

'What else you want to know?

'Wanking?

'Uh?

'*Not in public, you'll go to jail*!

'Hokay?'

Fielding, eyes down, cheeks aflame, timidly nodded.

Grossman screwed the note into a ball, threw it somewhere away.

'Fucking *goyim*,' he muttered. 'Everything they're got to have explained.'

Fielding shifted uncomfortably.

Grossman shot him a black glare.

'Yeah, and those suppers,' Grossman muttered. 'I know those suppers they give you. One bite, you're up half the night, you'll wish you never had it.'

And then chortled, pleased with his sagacity.

'Jesus,' Fielding silently moaned.

'What?' Grossman volleyed.

'Nothing,' Fielding said quickly.

'Nothing?' Grossman shouted. 'I'll give you nothing!'

Grossman drew back a hand as though to strike.

Fielding, wide-eyed, ducked and crouched.

Grossman openly sneered at the sight.

But quickly he calmed.

'Oh, another thing,' he said. 'Not with a broom handle. A cabbage, you wish to employ a cabbage, well, in certain circumstances. But a broom handle – never!'

Fielding promised with wide eyes never ever to have truck with a broom.

'Hokay,' said Grossman. 'Now you know it. The entire mysteries of life.'

And then fell to nodding, head shaking, muttered words.

'The clitoris. The vagina. The pudenda. The labia maximus, for God's sake. Jesus. I never heard such *dreck*. The simultaneous orgasm. Whoosh. Those fucking *goyim*. Who knows what they'll think up next?'

And then suddenly:

'You eat your lunch?'

Fielding's reply was inaudible.

'The turkey sandwiches!' Grossman shouted. 'What's the matter with you?'

Fielding again mumbled.

'What? Speak up! I can't hear a word!'

'Getzner stole them,' Fielding whispered, his eyes down shame at his feet.

'Getzner?' said Grossman. 'Who's this Getzner?'

'He's bigger than me,' Fielding whined.

Grossman stared at Fielding with disbelieving eyes, such words and shouts as he wished to deliver locked in his throat.

'He's bigger than everyone,' Fielding croaked, on the edge of tears.

Grossman's outrage, when it came, was truly massive.

'Getzner?' he howled. 'Getzner? Don't tell me Getzner! I don't want to hear any Getzner! For Getzner I'm rushing to the market? For Getzner I'm slaving my fingers to the bone? For Getzner I'm spending a fortune with doctors for my feet, which I've got such pains from standing half the night? Huh?'

Fielding quaked before Grossman's empurpled face.

'Getzner stole them,' Grossman mimicked, his thick lips twisted with sarcasm. 'So kick him one!' he shouted. 'Give him a *setz* in the *pilkess*, he won't walk straight for a month!'

Fielding trembled.

'What's the matter with you, you haven't got a *foot*?' Grossman roared. 'You haven't got an *eye*, you can't see where he keeps his *pilkess*?'

Fielding sobbed.

Grossman blinked, his disgust giving way to alarm.

'All right, all right,' he said. 'Stop that! That's enough! It's only a turkey sandwich, don't carry on like it was something different, like he stole your wallet as well.'

Fielding broke down in open blubbering.

Grossman stared, aghast.

'Shit!' he cried. 'You let him steal the wallet also? The pigskin? The *barmitzvah* gift?'

Fielding's face was a river of wetness and grief. Grossman had to look away.

'All right,' he said at last. 'All right. It happens. It happens. Nazis, what can you do? Come on there. That's enough. It's not the last pigskin wallet in the world what cost a hundred forty dollars, and that's after the discount. Come on there. Blow the nose. Better? Ha? Now wipe the face. That's right. Good.'

Grossman shook his head, pursed his lips.

'All right,' he said, Fielding now composed. 'I suppose you want now something to eat? Ha? Look over there. See? I bought you a nice cake. With chocolate, your favourite. Take a slice. Go on, a big one. But don't wolf! Eat nicely! And with it, please, a glass milk!'

Grossman, fingers laced over his stomach, watched as Fielding ate, from time to time shaking his head, letting out a mumbled 'I don't know,' a 'Sometimes I wonder,' a 'Where will it all end?' and in between each one a 'Whoosh!'

'Hokay,' said Grossman, when Fielding had finished. 'Now bring me the essay, what you wrote.'

Fielding handed it to him.

Grossman read.

'Ho ho,' he chortled, his eyes brightening at once. 'You've done a little William Faulkner here, that great Deep Southern phoney. Ho ho, yes, very nice. A brain you've got there, I won't deny. A real talent. Very nice. Except –' Grossman looked up sternly at Fielding '– this spelling! Gut Gott im Himmel! I've never seen such spelling! Look at this! You can't even spell *asshole*!'

Fielding's cheeks began to redden.

'Or *dick*!'

Fielding sniffed and snivelled.

'Not even *tush*!'

Fielding began once more to blubber.

'Oh, stop it!' Grossman shouted. 'Stop that crying! You're making me sick!'

Fielding sobbed gently, holding back the flood, calming down.

'Dat's better,' Grossman said. 'Dat's nice. Now come here. Come on, I'm not going to hit you. Come here.'

Fielding advanced with hesitant steps.

'Bend down.'

Grossman patted Fielding gently on the head.

'You're a good boy,' he said. 'A good boy. The spelling? Well, it's not such a big thing. Dostoyevsky couldn't spell either, look where he is today. Hokay? So calm down. You'll learn, you'll see, it's not so hard. Good. Now hand me there that towel, the feet I have soaked enough.'

Fielding looked elsewhere while Grossman dried, the sight of those white, aged, bunioned toes somehow too much for him, a mixture of obscene and the ultimately intimate. He was pleased when Grossman hid them away in battered felt slippers, pushed the tin tub to one side.

'Ah, dat's better,' said Grossman.

He smiled up at Fielding.

'Now fetch the fiddles,' he said.

Fielding, from a cupboard, brought out the cello, and from the shelf above, his violin.

'Hokay,' said Grossman, bringing his instrument expertly and quickly into tune. 'We'll begin a little Mendelssohn, to warm the fingers.'

Grossman bent at once with his bow. His tone rang out rich and deep, ringing around the room.

Fielding's violin was a flustered squeak.

'Tuck in, tuck in!' Grossman snapped. 'What for you think God gave you a chin?'

'Sorry,' Fielding apologized, quickly correcting his stance.

'All right now,' said Grossman. 'From the top.'

Fielding began again, but no less hesitant and clumsy.

'No, no!' Grossman roared. 'The elbow, the elbow! Not like that with the elbow!'

Grossman, to show him, surged ahead, bowing with passion, squeaky Fielding scurrying to keep up.

Grossman mopped his brow with an outsize handkerchief.

'We'll move now to the Brahms,' he said.

Fielding began, skittery and screechy.

Grossman shuddered at the sound.

'What's the matter with you?' he shouted. 'Don't you remember *anything*?'

He glared at Fielding, and was about once more to shout, but suddenly his mood altered.

'All right, all right,' he said. 'You want the doctor, the questions, the supper afterwards?'

Fielding timidly nodded.

'All right, all right. Big deal. We'll go. Hokay? You happy now?'

Fielding nodded and nodded, his whole face a rhapsodic smile.

'I don't know,' Grossman muttered. 'In the middle of Brahms, all he thinks is *shtupp*.'

Grossman sighed wearily.

And then was all at once businesslike, crisp.

'All right! The Bach! The Bach! We will play now the Bach!'

He looked up at Fielding, bow poised.

'Are you ready there?'

'Yes,' Fielding said.

'Then let us begin.'

Around them, unnoticed, the windows had darkened. The bright day had fled. Now the portals of night had opened outside.

Grossman and Fielding moved slowly into the Bach.

Grossman leading, Fielding quickly following, then together, locked as one, they moved into the timeless majesty of that bygone stately age.

Slowly the music swelled and grew.

Under his eyeglasses, Grossman silently wept.

Fielding's eyes were no less moist.

One sitting, one standing.

Weeping.

Bowing.

The pornographers together played.

Robert Redford, Robert Redford, Robert Redford, Robert Redford, Robert Redford, ROBert Redford, ROBert Redford, oh flex those jaw muscles, baby, you know the way you flick them, Robert, Robert, Robert, Robert, ROBert, ROBert, ROBert, and that thing you do with your lips, that slow pursing, oh honey, Robert, Robert, those cold clear blue eyes, Robert, Robert, ROBert, ROBert, ROBert, Rob, Rob, ROB, ROB, ROB, ROB ROB . . .

What is all this Robert Redford stuff?

It is eleven o'clock on a Tuesday morning, is what it is, a suburban Tuesday morning, for God's sake, which means that the kiddies, little Atticus and little

Samantha and little Norbert and little Hermione and little all the rest of them, are all tucked nicely away in their kinders and creches and day-care centres and schools . . .

Oh Robert, Robert, Rob, Rob, Rob, Rob . . .

. . . and all the darling hubbies are tucked away too, commuted off to the Big City, hustling, bustling, making a dollar, whisking up the wherewithal to put the bread on the table, baby needs new shoesies – Conferences! Meetings! – steeling themselves, this very minute, for yet another of those Heavy Lunches they're required to have, you know the kind, where those short-white-starchy-coated servitors are forever leaning in and splashing yet more Dom Perignon into your goblet . . .

OH ROB ROB ROB ROB ROB ROB –

. . . leaving these gorgeous young wives in this quiet suburb to their own devices.

And devices (gasp!) is the word!!!

There are about twenty of them here, twenty of these gorgeous, juicy, pampered-skin, sauna-toned, blush-lovely wives – What a salute to Motherhood! – wearing everything from minis to stretch pants – with real zippers that open right the way up – to fruit-picker designer denims with that big handy bib pocket that rides exactly in front of your bra-less liberated softly swinging nipple-ready young breasts . . .

Except for Darlene, of course!

That's Darlene out the front there!

On the zebra-patterned free-form divan!

ROB! ROB! ROB! ROB!

Of course that's not your real zebra there, it's your synthetic, one of those polysomethingorothers, man-made

– Conservationists rejoice! – except what they don't tell you is they have to melt down *at least* nineteen *damn zebras just to make one square yard of the damn stuff!*

Well, what the hell, who's looking at the fabric, all eyes are on darling Darlene, who is stretched out there wearing nothing at all but her natural-born softly golden pink skin and her long blonde hair in charming disarray – and yes, she's a real blonde too, although it is slightly darker down there – and everything is going jouncy and bouncy all over the place – O Clitoris Heaven! O Heavenly Right Stuff! – and matters must be coming to a head pretty soon, if I'm any judge.

'Rob!' cries Darlene. 'Rob . . . Rob . . .'

Just one long sobbing breath . . . ooooooooohhhh . . . then up she jumps, staunch professional that she is, holding aloft the actual device she has just so prettily demonstrated, and smiling too to beat the band, never mind the weariness those lovely limbs must be feeling.

'Anyone care to try?' she asks, beaming round the room. 'Come on, ladies. Don't be shy.'

But she doesn't even have to ask! Look at all those hands flying up! Everyone wants to try it! What a great group!

And now darling Darlene bends prettily down to this box she has on the floor, and then starts handing out these little brochures *– you said it! and not just with* diagrams *either, these are full-colour live-action* photographs! *– at the same time going into her sales pitch . . .*

'Ladies, when you invest in a Finger Pie Home Use Personal Entertainment Centre, you are investing not only in your personal pleasure, but in sound economics

> *too. Why, barely a week goes by without your Finger*
> *Pie going up and up and up!!!*

Fielding, in the crowd, saw a gun.
With the gun came a face.
Fielding knew that face.
They'd found him.
He was dead.
Shot dead in the street at three o'clock in the afternoon right outside his hotel, the gangster's murderous bullet sledgehammering straight into his throbbing heart, life's last blood spurting out through the Warner's Formfit bra, the frilly silk Jaegar blouse, the classic Chanel jacket; gushing crimson over the Gucci gloves, over and into the matching handbag, gushing and running and staining and soaking; the river of hot sticky redness in seconds rendering unreadable that which was within, his latest painstaking literary endeavour, a slap in the chops to that white-suited posturing phoney Tom Wolfe, shafted at last with his own exclamation point – Take that, Wolfe! Yarrr!!! – Fielding's copy the only copy in existence – he hadn't bothered making a carbon this time – for the good Mr Grossman of Grossman Press.

'No!' Fielding screamed. 'No!'

The aged couple about to board the cab at the kerb froze midstep. They were more than aged. The man wore a surgical neckbrace and stood propped on a crutch. The woman was in a wheelchair, or, more correctly, being assisted from it by a porter. Both exhibited that claypipe fragility a step from the grave.

Fielding bowled them aside like skittles.

'Go!' he screamed at the cabbie, spewing money in a torrent. 'For God's sake, go!'

The cab took off in a squeal of rubber.

Fielding lying flung full-length along the seat.

Heart hammering.

Silken panties sopping.

And shit the heel snapped clean off his left high-heeled black pump.

'Where to?' the cabbie asked.

Fielding gasped out the address.

And at last he managed to sit up.

He lit, with trembling hands, the first of a succession of rapid cigarettes.

He thought, 'I can't ever go back to that hotel.'

He thought, 'Good thing I put my money somewhere else.'

He thought, 'Ha ha, that aged couple.'

He thought, 'Wait a minute, hasn't that black car been behind us too long?'

He thought, 'Shit!'

'Shit!' Fielding cried.

'Somethin' up?' the cabbie asked.

Fielding was once again prone on the seat.

'I . . . I think we're being followed . . .' he gasped.

The cabbie wearily shook his head.

'Ho ho, you transvestites,' he said. 'Someone's always chasin' ya, right? OK, hold tight, lover. Here we go.'

Gears screamed and roared.

Tyres squealed.

Brakes slammed all around.

Crouched along the seat in total terror, his face thrust deep into the fart-foul vinyl, his eyes squeezed tight, Fielding quaked before imminent death.

Oh the sweet bounteous goodness of the earth that he had spurned, profligate and uncaring and heedless of speeding time, the grass, the sun, the sighing winds, the scudding cloud shadows over green rolling fields, the soft sound of trout rising in misty streams, the ceaseless miracle of fresh falling snow – Fielding saw them all now achingly clear and forever gone, denied him, lost, his to enjoy no more.

'Dear God in Heaven Above,' Fielding devoutly prayed. 'Oh let me but live and I promise never again to suggest to my good wife her participation in obscene and unnatural acts during Prime Time TV. Or spy on my daughter slipping in her Pantie Shields. Or on my son secretly jerking off into my best hat. Oh I'll be good. Oh please God, I won't even stand in the rose bushes in the dead of night with my cassette recorder and infra-red camera hoping for a glimpse of my stalwart decent neighbours doing that thing they sometimes do on top of the fridge.'

'Wake up, lover,' the cabbie cried. 'We're there.'

Fielding saw Grossman's grey building, the street in both directions safely normal, no black murderer's car in sight.

He saw that he was alive.

He hobbled out.

'Oh, lover?'

Fielding turned to stone, a sphincter-flick from dropping his whole load.

'Have a nice day.'

The elevator, of course, was out of order. Fielding dragged himself broken-heeled up the stairs. One flight up he passed a glass door and saw in reflection for the first time his true wretched state.

Fielding recoiled, aghast.

He was wet. He was soiled. He reeked of sweat and ordure. His bra had snapped, one fake breast sagging like a sack. Flesh bulged like goitres from stockings laddered front and back. A pink finger gaped obscenely from a torn Gucci glove.

But all that nothing compared to his face.

For here was the ultimate ogre, a gargoyle of horror.

Leprous powder rose in cracked blisters. Eyeliner ran black in channels of sweat. Lipstick stained like fiendish gore his teeth and cheeks and quivering wet chin. From one black-smudged staring eye a dislodged lash dangled like a creeping vile slug.

Fielding's face that of a harried pervert surprised in the middle of unspeakable acts.

'Why, Professor Fielding!' cried Miss Barthelmess, rising from her desk.

Fielding stood, red-faced and panting.

'Are you all right, Professor?'

She stepped towards him, blinking eyes huge with concern.

Fielding's breath was a toiling tractor.

Impossible to speak.

Miss Barthelmess advanced another worried step.

'Um, Mr Grossman's a little busy at the moment,' she said. Her eyes swum contrite with apology. 'But I'm sure he won't be long. Can I get you something? A cup of coffee?'

Fielding shook his bowed head.

'A glass of water?'

His eyes stayed down.

'Oh, dear,' said Miss Barthelmess, advancing in her concern yet another step.

Fielding stood.

Head down.

Shoulders slumped.

Defeated.

And then, for the first time in his adult life, he began openly to cry.

A first tear ran hot down his ravaged cheek.

Then another.

Another.

Fielding saw Fielding, broken and weeping, a dismembered clown.

In this hopeless building.

In this hopeless life.

His tears falling naked to the floor at his feet.
'Professor . . .?'
Fielding looked up.
Miss Barthelmess stood before him in her crisp white blouse and plain grey skirt and sensible flat-heeled shoes, not a step away.
Her hand on his arm, a gentle white dove.
'Professor . . .?' she said again.
Fielding looked up through his veil of tears.
Her lips hung open.
Her eyes were wide.
Her whole face seemed to tremble with sympathy and compassion.
Fielding felt his heart lurch with shame.
He began to turn away, to flee, disgraced to be seen by such youth and freshness and innocence, oh anywhere, anywhere, to escape those eyes.
But how? Where?
Fielding plunged his shame into Miss Barthelmess' shampoo-soft hair.
Oh distraught Fielding.
Wetting her sweet face with his foul tears.
Her eyes.
Her cheeks.
And suddenly – oh madness, madness – her lips.
Her innocent soft mouth.
But what was this?
Where Fielding expected nothing he met a hot whip.
The flicking serpent of Miss Barthelmess' tongue.
Darting and flying from a cave of winds.

Fielding reeled.
Staggered.
A crazed hand leaping to a breast.
As hers to his swelling crotch.
By accident?
His eyes sought hers.
Helpless?
Urgent?
A beseeching mystery.
Oh Miss Barthelmess, Miss Barthelmess!
Fielding fell in supplication to his knees.
Hands flying with dervish madness.
Her skirt.
Her tights.
Her pristine white cotton panties.
Down!
Gone!
And beneath –
Oh adorable, adorable.
A cleft apricot.
A honeyed peach.
An orbed mount made soft with the merest floss.
Fielding, in a lifetime of looking, both real and imagined, had never seen such perfection.

Frenzied, maddened, aswoon with love, Fielding anointed her there with a million kisses, gentle, lapping, and then bolder, the cleft itself, and deeper, her gorgeous button, tiny but upright like a knot in silky string, each lapping flick releasing a shuddering moan, her hands in his hair at first restraining, and then – deeper, bolder – insisting otherwise, guiding, pleading, fierce with want.

Fielding rose from her one wet mouth to her other.

And she no less engaged, tearing up his skirt, ripping down his silken panties, finding him, holding him, squeezing and squeezing, playing him to the very brink of madness with her musical hand.

Fielding was beyond ecstasy.

'Oh Miss Barthelmess, Miss Barthelmess!' his galloping heart sang. 'I don't care about my wife, my children, about anyone or anything, it's just you, I want you forever, I don't care if I die!'

'Oh hurry, hurry! Now, now!' sang back Miss Barthelmess, expiring with her eyes. 'Oh yes! Yes!'

But where?

On the floor?

No.

Here.

On the desk.

On Miss Barthelmess' neat and tidy desk.

Quickly.

Like this.

Ah . . .

Oh . . .

She opened.

He pressed in.

Her lovely legs over his shoulders.

A starfish.

A dream.

Oh she was wetter and tighter and hotter and deeper and more gorgeous than he had ever envisioned anyone in his wildest fantasies, he was dying, he was dying, but exquisitely, slowly, oh he wanted everything, please don't let it stop, her moans and cries, each stroke trembling on the very brink, but not yet, not yet, his head popping and exploding –

Popping?

Exploding?

Fielding, mid-stroke, looked quickly up.

At Grossman, dancing in, flashbulbs flaring a mile a minute on the massive black camera before his thick-lipped juicy smile.

'Oh don't stop, Professor, don't stop, plizz!' cried the pornographer. 'Ve is also doing picture books!'

More about Penguins
and Pelicans

For further information about books
available from Penguin please write to
Dept EP, Penguin Books Ltd,
Harmondsworth, Middlesex UB7 ODA.

In the U.S.A.: For a complete list of books
available from Penguin in the United
States write to Dept DG, Penguin Books,
299 Murray Hill Parkway, East
Rutherford, New Jersey 07073.

In Canada: For a complete list of books
available from Penguin in Canada write to
Penguin Books Canada Ltd, 2801 John
Street, Markham, Ontario L3R 1B4.

In Australia: For a complete list of books
available from Penguin in Australia write
to the Marketing Department, Penguin
Books Australia Ltd, P.O. Box 257,
Ringwood, Victoria 3134.

In New Zealand: For a complete list of books
available in New Zealand write to the
Marketing Department, Penguin Books
(N.Z.) Ltd, P.O. Box 4019, Auckland 10.

Dirty Friends

Stories by Morris Lurie

In Tangier a lonely poet confronts the ugliest truth . . . in Greece a millionaire makes a dazzling escape . . . in Yugoslavia a marriage falters . . . in Melbourne a friendship shows its other face . . .

Wherever he is (Switzerland, New York), whomever he addresses (a fancy mistress, a wry Jewish uncle), Morris Lurie displays that uncanny mixture of humour and compassion which has won him an international audience.

'Mr Lurie is a gifted impressionist, he arranges scraps of dialogue, reverie and observation in a volatile mixture that bubbles with life . . .'
The New York Times Books Review

'Lurie has that kind of acute appreciation of social farce that tots up to a real observation of the styles of the culture.'
Malcolm Bradbury, *Guardian*

Flying Home

A novel by Morris Lurie

Leo Axelrod, blocked painter, successful illustrator, lonely and alone in England, asks a girl to come with him to Greece. He doesn't know anything about her, he doesn't even know her name, but amazingly she says yes.

They set off joyously, in a second-hand red Mini packed with luggage and plans, but they are not alone in the car. For Leo's parents are there too, and his grandfather, the three loveless ghosts Leo has brought with him from Australia.

And Marianne has her ghosts too.

For children by Morris Lurie

Arlo the Dandy Lion, illustrated by Brett Colquhoun (Young Puffin)

The Twenty-Seventh Annual African Hippopotamus Race, illustrated by Elizabeth Honey (Young Puffin)

Toby's Millions, illustrated by Arthur Horner (Puffin & Kestrel)

Woman in a Lampshade

Elizabeth Jolley

In this masterly collection of stories, Elizabeth Jolley has created a splendid array of characters, all of whom fail to achieve the expected. Her stories are sometimes slyly comic, sometimes disturbing – but always they are written with a delicacy and compassion as moving as the characters themselves.

'The depth of understanding in her short stories is often disturbing. Sometimes the humour, or the celebration, seems almost a desperate counter to despair and the full burden of that understanding . . .'
Thomas Shapcott, *Westerly*

Elizabeth Jolley's stories 'are about very simple people, but with deep human sensitivity, and their dreams, though hopeless, put haloes around the contours of everyday drabness.'
A. R. Chisholm, Melbourne *Age*

Mr Scobie's Riddle

A novel by Elizabeth Jolley

Mr Scobie's arrival at the nursing home of St Christopher and St Jude – and into the clutches of Matron Hyacinth Price – is accidental. Self-educated and still preserving the gift of idyllic memory and wish, Mr Scobie stands apart from the others. For long-term resident and eccentric, Miss Hailey, he represents a kindred spirit; for Matron Price – a lady of questionable practices – the latest victim . . .

But unwittingly Mr Scobie has some recourse – his very simple riddle. Its answer – an ancient commonplace – jolts Matron Price.

Yet it is Mr Scobie's nephew, Hartley, and the group of nocturnal poker players, who ultimately change Matron Price's establishment . . .

'Her writing is splendid, her characters various, her humour delicious.'
                Nancy Keesing, *Australian Book Review*

'Elizabeth Jolley is a major figure in recent Australian writing.'
                Thomas Shapcott, *Westerly*

Fly Away Peter

David Malouf

For three very different people brought together by their love for birds, life on the Queensland coast in 1914 is the timeless and idyllic world of sandpipers, ibises and kingfishers.

In another hemisphere civilization rushes headlong into a brutal conflict. Life there is lived from moment to moment.

Inevitably, the two young men – sanctuary owner and employee – are drawn to the war, and into the mud and horror of the trenches of Armentières. Alone on the beach, their friend Imogen, the middle-aged wildlife photographer, must acknowledge for all three of them that the past cannot be held.

'the continuities of nature are set against the obscenities of war . . . to construct a memorable book'

Sunday Telegraph, London

'The novel of a poet without a single trace of overwriting.'

Daily Telegraph, London

Child's Play

David Malouf

In the streets of an ordinary Italian town,
the people go about their everyday lives.
In an old apartment block above them, a
young man pores over photographs and
plans, dedicated to his life's most important
project.

Day by day, in imagination, he is
rehearsing for his greatest performance.
Yet when his moment comes, nothing
could have prepared him for what
happens . . .

'one of the most effective and penetrating
studies of the mind and being of a fanatic'
Financial Times, London

'written with the beautiful clarity and
sharp edges of cut crystal'
Sunday Telegraph, London

Included with this novella are two stort stories,
Eustace *and* The Prowler